C000097258

CONTENTS

craig zerf

Emily Shadowhunter Book 5 PROPHECY

CHAPTER 1

Father Dubois knelt down next to the body, crossing himself as he did.

'Did anyone call the *Gendarmes*?' he asked.

'Yes, Father,' answered *monsieur* Petit. 'I called the police. He is on his way. He had to finish lunch first.'

The priest nodded. Lunch was important. After all, the body was going nowhere and there was little the *Gendarme* could do about it. But to spoil a good meal was a crime in itself.

The girl lying on the ground was pale. As pale as a shroud. Unnaturally so, even for a corpse.

And this was the second one in as many weeks.

The priest mumbled a prayer under his breath as he inspected the girl's wounds. The cause of death was obvious.

Her throat had been viciously torn open as if by a wild animal.

Father Dubois knew exactly what had killed the young woman.

This wanton destruction was the mark of the true feeder. Because, contrary to popular belief, they did not leave neat twin punctures as so often portrayed in the movies.

No, they ravened on their victims, ripping into them with an insatiable blood lust.

Worse than the most vicious of animals.

Evil personified.

Vampire.

The priest took out his cell phone and dialled a number. A number he had hoped to never use, even though it had been in his possession for over ten years.

It was answered on the second ring.

'Muller.'

'Most Holy Knight,' greeted the father. 'My name is father Dubois of the Voire parish. We have a problem.'

And he told the Knight of the Holy See about the two attacks.

'The Voire parish, you say?' enquired Muller.

'Yes, most Holy.'

'I know the area. In the Dordogne?'

'That is correct, most Holy.'

'I have some loose ends to tie up, but I will be there in two or three days. However, father Dubois, you are in luck. There is someone I know who lives in the Voire region. I will text you their details. Go straight to them. Tell them, Dietz Muller, Knight of the Holy See sent you. Tell them of the attacks.'

'I will be done, most Holy.'

'Oh, and father.'

'Yes.'

'When you meet them, be strong, do not let your fear overcome you. And above all, show respect, these are beyond doubt the most lethal beings you will ever meet. And they may not be that happy to see you.'

The knight rang off.

And it was with great trepidation that father Dubois noted that Muller had referred to them as *Beings* ... not *Humans*.

CHAPTER 2

Emily leaned the push bike up against the barn, picked up her basket of goods and walked to the house, entering through the back door, straight into the large farmhouse kitchen.

Troy stood up from the table to greet her.

'Steak?' he asked.

Emily opened the straw bag and took out a massive cut of beef. Enough to make a meal for a family of eight. Or a dinner for a werewolf and his mate.

There were no vegetables.

The two had been living in the Dordogne for just over a year. The farmhouse was large but basic. Running hot and cold water, fireplaces for warmth, old but solid furniture. A radio, but no television.

Nestled in amongst rows of grape vines, it had once been a winery, but now the vats lay idle.

After their last great battle against the vampires, resulting in the loss of Bastian, William, Sylvian and most of the pack, Emily and Troy had left the United Kingdom and headed for the rural environs of the French Dordogne.

It was with surprise that Emily had discovered that both William and Sylvian had left all they owned to her in their wills. Countless millions in cash, gold, jewels and antiques. As well as numerous properties dotted around the United Kingdom and Europe.

If you added this largess to the Institute's funds that she controlled, it made Emily one of the wealthiest people in Europe.

But the money meant little to either her or Troy.

The simple farmhouse was all they needed.

They knew they were hiding from responsibility. Their planned period of R & R had stretched out to become a way of life, and now they lived day to day. Revelling in their wolfen forms by night, running free through the surrounding oak and chestnut forests. Remaining human by day.

Eating. Sleeping. Making love.

And not thinking about vampires.

Troy used a kitchen knife to slice the haunch of beef into huge steaks while Emily heated a cast iron grill on the stove. But before Troy could begin his cook up, both Emily and he stopped what they were doing and cocked their heads to one side.

'Bicycle,' said Emily.

Troy sniffed the air. 'Male. Stranger.'

Emily turned the stove off and the two of them walked to the front door, about them a definite air of readiness. Coiled springs.

9

Tension.

They listened and waited as the bicycle came to a halt. They heard the stand being kicked down followed by footsteps.

As the visitor approached the front door, Troy whipped it open.

Father Dubois flinched back. In front of him stood a young male. Well over six foot tall, perhaps two hundred and thirty pounds of ripped muscle. Long dark hair, short beard and moustache.

And eyes of golden yellow.

Behind him, one of the most beguiling looking females he had ever seen. Tall, slender, long blonde hair and flawless, pale skin. Unlike the male, her eyes were an impossible green.

As green as an Irish lover's grave.

And the raw power that radiated off the two of them made him feel as if he was being scorched with fire. It was a physical, palpable thing. An aura of supreme authority.

Such was their obvious superiority, he had to force himself not to kneel in their presence. Instead, he mumbled a quick Hail Mary to give himself the strength to face them.

'Father,' greeted the female, her voice low, husky yet musical. 'Please, come in.'

The powerful young man raised an eyebrow as if surprised at the girls welcome, then he stood aside and ushered the priest in, closing the door behind him.

The girl led them through to the kitchen and she sat down at the large, oak table.

'Something to drink?' she asked. 'Tea?'

'Perhaps something a little stronger?' requested the priest.

Troy opened a cupboard, took out a bottle and showed it to the priest for his approval.

The father registered what it was and nodded his thanks, while at the same time trying not to gawk open mouthed at the treasure the young man held in his hand. It was a bottle of 1762 Gautier Cognac. He was no specialist, but he knew that a bottle like that would retail for over a hundred thousand dollars. He would have swooned had he known that the young couple had over a hundred more bottles of the liquor, courtesy of one of Sylvian's private cellars.

The young man casually sloshed some into a trio of tumblers. Treating the liquid gold like it was Kool-Aid.

He slid one across the table to the priest and then extended his hand.

'Name's Troy,' he said.

The father took his hand, noting the strength and the rough callouses. The hands of a working man. The grip firm, but nowhere close to how hard the man was obviously capable of squeezing. He felt no need for childish games of macho posturing. His enormous strength was blatantly obvious.

The girl offered her hand next. 'Emily,' she

11

said. 'Some call me, Em.'

The priest blinked when he took her hand. The brief contact told him that the girl's strength surpassed the male's by an order of magnitude. She shook his hand with great care, as if she might inadvertently crush his bones if she didn't concentrate on not doing so.

'So, priest,' said Troy. 'Talk to us.'

Father Dubois took a tentative sip of the cognac and sighed. Ambrosia.

'I was sent by Knight of the Holy See, Dietz Muller.'

Dubois was about to continue, explaining the why's and what's, but before he could, a wave of fear crashed over him and he saw Emily's eyes change from deep green to a vivid scarlet.

At the same time, Troy growled. A deep, visceral sound that connected directly with Dubois' amygdala, speaking to him on a primal level. Warning him of life-threatening danger.

It was an utterly inhuman sound.

He dropped his cognac, spilling a couple of thousand dollars' worth of alcohol onto the kitchen table as his fingers fumbled with fear and his brain went into freefall.

He clutched at the crucifix hanging around his neck and mumbled a prayer.

And then, just like that, the fear receded. Em touched his shoulder.

'Sorry, father,' she apologised. 'We mean no harm; it was simply a shock to hear that name after so many months. Tell us, why did Dietz send you?'

So, father Dubois told them of the two victims.

Neither spoke for a while, then Troy asked. 'Just out of interest, how did Dietz know where we were, we didn't tell anyone?'

Dubois chuckled. 'There are almost twenty million Catholics in France. It is impossible to keep any secrets from the church. Particularly if someone like Dietz Muller is looking for you.'

Emily sighed. 'Our vacation is over, isn't it?'

Troy leaned over the table and kissed her. 'Yes,' he replied. 'I'm afraid it is.' He turned to the priest. 'Father, take us to see the bodies.'

CHAPTER 3

Tag put his finger through the hole in his shirt and sighed. He hated getting shot. Especially when he was wearing his fancy duds.

The man who shot him stared open mouthed at the huge Jamaican, then he pointed his pistol at him and fired again, pulling the trigger until the slide racked back. Eleven rounds of 9mm shredded the rest of the big man's shirt and covered his torso in blood.

Tag took a step forward, grabbed his assailant by the neck and squeezed. The attacker batted ineffectually at his arm, but the big man was as strong as ten normal people. This, plus the fact that he was almost impossible to kill, made the ex-yardie an opponent of note.

'That's a silk shirt, asswipe,' growled Tag as he increased pressure until, with a sharp crack, the man's spine shattered. Then he dropped the limp body to the floor and turned to his compatriot.

'Was that the last one?' he asked.

Dietz Muller, vampire hunter and Knight of the Holy See, nodded. 'The last familiar. Now we just need to find the chief bloodsucker, dispatch it, and our work here is done.'

Tag stripped off his blood drenched shirt, dropped it to the floor, drew a pair of massive pistols from his waistband and checked the loads. Each carried ten rounds of silver coated .50 caliber Action Express in an extended mag. Tag had always been a believer in the saying - go large or go home.

'Have you got a spare shirt?' asked Muller.

'Sure,' replied Tag. 'In the car. But I'm not putting it on yet. Only got a couple left.'

Muller nodded his agreement. The knight carried a sawn-off, double barreled shotgun in one hand and a silver sword in the other. Like Tag's weapons, the shotgun was loaded with silver coated slugs. The precious metal an anathema to any vampire.

Muller led the way, treading softly as they crossed the room and headed for the doorway that opened to the basement.

The house wasn't what one might expect when it came to an immortal blood sucking fiend. Middle income, neatly trimmed garden, gas grill out back and a Prius in the driveway. But that was due to the fact that this was a new vampire. Barely weeks old. Not yet having been able to take advantage of decades of long-term investments and sales of antiques to amass any large store of wealth.

But even a young vamp can be dangerous. Their saliva is poisonous, and their ability to glamor humans, while still relatively weak, was strong enough for it to have recruited two familiars as servants.

And, to be fair, the familiars had tried their best to protect their master while it slept away the daylight hours. But after failing to kill the unkillable Tag, they found themselves at the end of a very short journey. One that concluded with both of them being wiped out by the big man.

Oh well, easy come, easy go. Natural selection.

Muller pushed the door open and crept down the stairs, weapons ready. This wasn't going to be easy, as they wanted to question the newly turned creature before destroying it. It was important to find out who had turned them. Because only an elder can actively turn a human. And elders were extremely dangerous and needed to be hunted down at all costs.

But first, obviously, they needed to be tracked down.

Contrary to popular belief, vampires do not sleep in coffins. In fact, strictly speaking, the older one's do not sleep at all. It is only the newly turned that need any down time. And this is always taken during the hours of daylight. Because, ultraviolet light will genuinely ruin a bloodsucker's day. Terminally.

Muller gestured towards the large, four poster double bed in the center of the room. The new vampire had clearly decided that, despite its previously pedestrian white-collar existence, it would at very least kit it's boudoir out in a fashion that befit a true creature of the night.

There was no other way to describe the basement-become-bedroom than, High Gothic. Everything from black candles in a huge floor standing candelabra, to carved stone gargoyles perched in the corners of the room.

Dark kitsch.

Muller and Tag approached the bed from opposite sides and, on Muller's signal, they tore aside the drapes.

The bed was empty.

The vampire struck Tag like a combine harvester, launching from the shadows in the corner of the room. Fangs and talons slashing and biting and tearing at him. Blood sprayed from deep cuts in Tag's chest and arms as he struggled to bring one of his weapons to bear. But the vamp was too fast for the big man.

Fortunately, before it could strip Tag to the bone, Muller's sword flashed out, catching the bloodsucker a glancing blow to its throat, opening up a gaping wound, but not removing the head.

The vamp fell to the floor, spitting and growling.

Tag used the respite to grab its arms, wrench them behind its back and bind them tight with a length of stout silver chain. Then he wrapped another length of chain around its ankles, pulling hard enough to cut into its flesh.

The vampire screamed in agony as the silver burned through its undead skin. Muller cuffed it across its face hard enough to slam its head into the floor.

Then he took out a silver flask and held it in front of the vamp's eyes. 'Quiet,' he said. 'Or I'll pour this Holy Water on your face and watch it eat your flesh.'

The vampire, a young female that appeared to be in her late twenties, flinched back. Normally any vampire would scoff at being threatened with Holy Water, for it had little to no effect on them. But most had heard of sergeant Dietz Muller of the Holy See. A knight whose faith was so strong that if he cast Holy Water upon the evil – it burned them with fire.

But she wasn't sure if the stories were mere rumor, or based on fact. Truth be told, it seemed unlikely.

'Now, this is how things are going to proceed,' said Muller. 'I shall ask a question. You shall answer. If you hesitate, or if I find the answer unsatisfactory – Holy Water. However, if you cooperate fully and truthfully.' He held up the silver sword. 'A swift and honorable death.'

The vampire hissed as the chains continued to burn her.

'First, who turned you?' asked Muller.

The vampire stared at him, unblinking. Then she sneered.

The room reverberated with the loud booming sound of Tag's Desert Eagles discharging. Both of the vamp's knees exploded as the fifty caliber rounds destroyed them.

Muller sighed and stared at the big man.

Tag shrugged. 'Sorry,' her mumbled. 'I know it was Holy Water time, but I got pissed. After all, she did cut me up real bad.'

The girl let out a long-drawn-out wail of pain as they waited a few minutes for her knees to heal up.

After they had regenerated, Muller repeated his question. She still didn't answer, but this time, neither did she sneer.

Progress. Albeit small.

The knight uncorked his flask.

'Last chance.'

No reaction.

He tipped the flask up and released a single drop of the liquid onto the vampire's forehead.

'The power of Christ compels me,' he proclaimed as the water fell.

The vampire reacted like she had received a massive electric shock. Thrashing about, gnashing her teeth and grunting in agony.

Tag watched in morbid fascination as the tiny drop of water melted the vampire's flesh and bone, sizzling and popping as it scoured across her formally flawless skin.

Usually, the creature would heal almost instantly from such a wound, but the Sanctity of Muller's offering did not allow that to happen. The raw wound sizzled and bubbled, slowly etching deeper and deeper as it visited massive amounts of pain upon the evil monster.

'That was one drop,' stated the knight. 'One tiny drop. Next time I will up-end the entire flask onto your face. Now, talk.'

The vamp spent the next ten minutes spilling her guts.

And then the sword fell.

CHAPTER 4

The village of Voire didn't have a mortuary. It didn't even have a town doctor. But the *gendarme* had gotten around that lack by simply storing the two bodies on a large table in the town butcher's walk-in fridge. Next to the cuts of beef and chicken.

The authorities were supposed to collect the corpses any day now, but with the usual Gallic penchant for procrastination, that time had not yet transpired.

In a token nod to hygiene, the butcher had pinned up a plastic sheet between the bodies and the produce. Problem solved.

Troy leaned over the bodies and sniffed. 'Vampire,' he growled.

Both victims were female. Girls in their late teens. Both had their throats viciously torn open and their pallor, even in death, showed they had been totally exsanguinated.

Emily ran her finger over the wounds. 'Different attackers,' she deduced. 'See the bite marks. This one,' she pointed. 'Most likely female. This one, male. Much bigger. Longer fangs. Older.' She turned to Dubois. 'Show us where the bodies were found.'

The priest nodded and then shrugged. 'It has been a while. A week since the first murder, and two days since the second. I doubt you will find any actionable clues.'

Emily looked at the priest and he flinched under her gaze.

'We shall be the judge of that, father,' she informed him. 'Now, show us. Time marches on and these monsters will strike again, soon. Mark my words.'

CHAPTER 5

'I hate this stupid car,' grumbled Tag.

Muller shrugged. 'It's fast, cheap to run and it's also the only one the Vatican will give us.'

'I never trust any car that I weigh more than,' insisted the big man.

Muller didn't answer. He was used to Tag complaining about the car. But this was Italy, and if they requisitioned a huge 4x4 or a Mercedes saloon, they would stand out. Now, with the small Fiat, they blended in with the locals wherever they went. Of course, as soon as they debussed, they stood out like dog's balls on a blanket. Expensive tailored suits, handmade shoes, an unmistakable aura of danger and twin thousand-yard stares.

Plus, the fact they both moved like predators. Carnivores roaming the savannah. Leopards seeking prey.

Sharks amongst a shoal of bait fish.

These were men who dealt in death for a living. And it was obvious.

The crucifixes they both openly wore did little to dispatch those fears.

Muller pulled over, stopping the car in a vague approximation of parallel parking. The front of the car nestled up against the rear of the next car and the back stuck out a couple of feet into the road.

Tag had long since stopped advising the Knight on his seeming inability to park correctly. After all, the Italians seemed to find road rules a relatively arbitrary recommendation, as opposed to an actual law. And in all fairness, Tag thought that attitude was pretty cool.

'This is the address,' said Muller as he squeezed out of the car and walked around to the trunk to get his jacket and weapons.

Tag followed suit, donning a new shirt at the same time.

The only major difference in their attire was the fact that Muller wore a lightweight bullet proof vest, whereas Tag went *au naturel*. Being shot hurt, but apart from that it had no lasting effect on the big man.

Not counting the ruined shirts, of course.

'Now this is more like it,' noted Tag as he looked at the residence they had arrived at.

The manicured garden was visible through a wrought iron fence. As was the house. A hotel sized Baroque Palazzo. All arched windows, pillars and water features.

If you were looking for it, and the two vampire hunters were, it was obvious that every window was covered with heavy drapes.

There were also two armed guards at the gate, both seated inside an open fronted guard house. One of them was smoking. The other, eating a sausage that was so redolent of garlic it made Tags eye's water, even from twenty feet away.

'I thought vamps didn't like garlic,' he murmured to Muller.

'Why?'

Tag shrugged. 'Just thought it. Isn't that what everyone says?'

'Maybe,' admitted the knight. 'But then everyone most likely has never actually seen a real vampire.'

'True. So, what now?'

'We could scout the place first. Check if the bloodsucker was telling the truth before we go in.'

'Nah,' disagreed the big Jamaican. 'There's no way she was lying. Never seen someone in such pain. She spoke the truth, bet my life on it.'

'I reckon you're correct,' concurred Muller. 'In that case, let's ask nicely if they can let us in.'

'And if they don't?'

'We kill them and let ourselves in,' answered Muller, as he tucked his crucifix inside his shirt.

CHAPTER 6

'Father,' said Emily. 'Thank you for bringing us here, now I advise you to leave.'

Dubois looked puzzled. 'Why?'

Troy grinned. 'Things are about to get weird,' he said. 'We need to look for clues. Anything that may give us a lead. And with the time that has passed, the only way for us to be able to do that is to use our ... enhanced senses, shall we say.'

'Magic?'

Emily shook her head. 'Not really. How much did Muller actually tell you about Troy and I?'

'He said you had the knowledge to help with these murders,' answered the priest. 'He said you knew about vampires and had worked with him before. I assumed you had something to do with the Vatican and the Knights of the Holy See.'

'Partly true,' acknowledged Em. 'But we have no connection with the church. Look, if you insist on staying, the best way to explain is simply to show you. But I warn you, your life will never be the same again. Are you prepared for that?'

Dubois nodded. 'Information is power,' he said. 'I will not shy away from anything that might help me fight this evil that stalks our land.'

Em nodded and then turned to Troy. 'Do it.'

The young man checked that there was no one around and he started to disrobe.

Dubois took a step backwards, but before he could ask why Troy was taking his clothes off, Em held up her hand to stay him.

As Troy stripped, he passed each item of clothing to Emily, who folded it neatly and placed it on the fence that ran along the stretch of road where the most recent victim's body had been discovered.

Dubois couldn't help but notice the naked young man in front of him seemed to have been constructed out of steel and leather. His muscles were so ripped that he looked like some sort of model for an anatomical lecture at a medical school. Rock hard muscles that were obviously forged outside of any gym. Long limbed, rangy and defined to the point of impossibility.

But before he could fully register Troy's physical prowess, Dubois's eyes started watering. It was as if the physical form in front of him was melting and reforming. Light bent and a shimmering wave of color rippled across his vision. He rubbed his eyes with the heels of his hands in an attempt to clear his sight – and when he opened his eyes again …

'Holy mother of God,' exclaimed the priest as he took two hurried steps backwards, stumbled over his own feet and fell to the floor.

Because there was no longer a young man standing in front of him.

Instead, he saw a wolf the size of a horse.

It's fur as black as a moonless night, its eyes still the same golden yellow that Troy's were, teeth the size of daggers and claws like sharpened meat hooks.

Then it growled. And Dubois felt like someone had taken hold of his amygdala and connected directly with his primal self, sending him a message.

And the message was – beware. You are in the presence of the ultimate predator.

The very top of the food chain.

Werewolf.

CHAPTER 7

'Hey, guard people,' Tag yelled at the two sentries. 'Can we come in? We wanna kill your blood sucking master, that okay with you?'

Muller shook his head and sighed. Something he tended to do quite a lot since he had started working with the huge Jamaican. What had started off as a few weeks of sightseeing, rest and recuperation after their last great battle in London, had turned into a full-time vampire hunting partnership that had been going over a year now.

And in all fairness, Tag was very good at what he did. The only problem was his overwhelming penchant for getting up in people's faces. An obvious habit carried over from his days as a street thug in London. He believed that the only real way to get people's attention and respect was to go at them like a bullet out of a gun.

The pair of guards stared at the big man like he was insane. Then the one shook his head.

'No, vattene. Non sei benvenuto qui. Idiota.'

Both of them drew their pistols.

Tag turned to Muller. 'What he say?'

'He said no,' translated the knight. 'And he called you an idiot.'

Tag shrugged. 'Oh well, I tried.' He pulled out one of his Desert Eagles, removed an oversized suppressor from his jacket pocket, screwed it on while the sentries regarded him with disbelieving expressions, and shot both of them in the face. 'There,' he said. 'That's for having an evil, murdering SOB for a boss.'

Then he removed the suppressor, pocketed it, replaced his pistol in his waistband, walked up to the wrought iron gate, spat on his hands, grabbed hold of it and started to apply some pressure.

Muller watched as the big man took the strain and, slowly, ripped the massive gate from its hinges.

Tag had always been a strong man. And that was before the mad professor had juiced him up with a potion that had initially killed him, then brought him back to life as a near immortal. Subsequently, the Prof had gone totally over the top and used Tag as an unkillable experimental human lab rat, plying him with a raft of potentially deadly concoctions to measure their effects.

And the one effect had been gifting the big man with superhuman strength.

As was blatantly apparent when he tore the huge gate off its mountings and cast it into the road.

'Come on,' he said to Muller. 'Let's go do some good.'

The two hunters strode up the crushed marble driveway towards the front door, drawing their respective weapons as they did.

'Look, Tag,' said Muller. 'Shooting those two men like that, was that absolutely necessary?'

'What should I have done?'

'I'm not sure, it's just, well, you didn't even try to give them an alternative.'

'Muller, my friend, they had their guns out, they work for a vamp and we needed to get past them. There was no way things were going down in a peaceful fashion. No matter how much we would have liked them to.'

'True. But be careful when we get into the house. There could be servants that are innocent with no idea they're actually working for a lord of the dark.'

Tag nodded. 'Okay, boss. I get it. No more shooting people inna face.'

'Unless you have to,' concluded Muller.

'Unless I have to,' agreed Tag.

By now they had arrived at the door.

'Should I knock?' asked the big man.

Muller nodded.

Tag took a run up and smashed through the oaken doors like they were Hollywood break-aways.

Muller allowed himself a quiet chuckle. Sometimes it was useful having a human battering ram as a hunting partner.

The hunters found themselves in a large entrance hall. It was your standard, no expense spared elder bloodsucker décor. Old masters on the walls, crystal chandeliers, Persian carpets, dim lighting and rubber backed drapes on all the windows.

There was likely to be a bevy of familiars. Depending on how paranoid the vamp was, those familiars could include as many as ten protectors or as little as two. There was often a cleaner, butler, driver and gardener. Vampires had no need of a chef.

A young woman entered the entrance hall via one of the side doors, obviously coming to check on the commotion. She was dressed in a classic maid's outfit. Taking one look at the intruders, she squealed and cowered against the wall.

'Now, you see,' said Muller, gesturing towards the terrified girl. 'This is one of those cases where it's not necessary to shoot anyone in the face.'

'Fine,' replied Tag. 'I get it.'

They turned their backs on the girl and started to proceed up the stairs, guessing that the master of the house would be in one of the main suites on the next floor.

As they walked away, the girl pulled up her skirt to reveal a thigh-holster, drew a compact Glock pistol and started firing.

Two rounds struck Muller. Both of them were

defeated by his body armor. The next three rounds hit Tag, punching into his left arm and shoulder.

'Dammit,' he shouted as he trained his Desert Eagle on the girl and pulled the trigger twice. Both rounds struck her in the chest, picking her up, throwing her across the room and painting the wall with her blood. 'You see,' he yelled at Muller. 'I should have shot her inna face.'

Muller frowned. 'Sorry,' he apologized. 'Who would have thought?'

'Me,' snapped Tag. 'I would have thought. Anyone who works for a vampire is bad news. And don't give me that – they might not know their master is a blood sucking monster. When your boss is mortally allergic to sunlight, doesn't eat anything except human blood and is a thousand years old – you gotta be terminally stupid to assume he is anything but a vampire.'

Muller didn't argue. After all, Tag was mostly correct. But, as a member of the Holy Church, Muller's job as a hunter was at odds with killing humans. He understood that all familiars had to be exterminated along with their masters, but it pained him nonetheless.

So, he allowed Tag his rave, and then led the way up the stairs, keeping his shotgun ready as now any form of surprise was well blown.

As they reached the landing, someone kicked open one of the doors leading off the corridor and opened up with a sub machine gun. Fortunately, they fired too soon, snatching at the trigger and pulling their aim high. The bullets stitched a line of potential death cross the wall above the hunter's heads.

Muller's shotgun boomed in response, punching the attacker back into the room. With practiced fingers, the knight reloaded his sawn-off double barrel.

Tag saw another door start to open and he fired into it, the huge .50 caliber rounds smashing through and dispatching the assailant in a welter of blood and bone chips.

Muller's shotgun boomed again, cutting down two uniformed men armed with pistols. Reloading swiftly, he fired again, ensuring that the men were dead.

'End of the corridor,' he shouted.

Tag nodded his agreement. At the end of the long corridor were a set of intricately carved double doors. Whoever resided behind those was obviously either a guest of note, or the Master himself.

Making their way down the corridor, they kicked open doors and cleared rooms as they went. They came across one more familiar. Kitted out in a dress suit and bow tie he was most likely the butler. He also carried an M16. But before he could crank any rounds off, Tag shot him twice. In the face.

'Time to do your battering ram thing again,' said Muller.

Tag grinned, pushed his pistols back into his belt and launched himself at the double doors. He struck them at full speed to the accompaniment of a loud cracking sound. Unfortunately, it was the sound of his right arm and shoulder breaking against the oak covered steel doors.

Falling to the floor he started cussing. A long uninterrupted string of every swear word he could think of. Then he made a few up.

A couple of minutes later his remarkable gift had ensured he was a hundred percent again.

'That did not work out like it was meant to,' he stated.

Muller studied the door closely, looking for any structural weaknesses.

'Maybe you could melt the locks out with Holy Water,' suggested Tag.

The knight didn't bother answering. Finally, he nodded and looked up. 'That door is impenetrable,' he said.

'Now what?'

'You think you could smash your way through an interconnecting wall instead?' asked the knight.

Tag shrugged. 'If it was only one brick thick. I doubt this old house is dry walled.'

'Fine, let's go into this adjacent room and try.'

'Okay.'

The two men proceeded to the next room. Firstly, they moved the bed aside, giving Tag a free run at the wall. Then Muller loaded his shotgun with solid slugs and Tag checked his mags were full.

Next, before the big man hit the wall, they marked out a two-foot circle about four feet from the ground and emptied their weapons into it, blasting off the plaster and chipping into the brick structure beneath.

As soon as they finished, they reloaded and Tag set himself.

Grunting with effort he ran full tilt into the wall, hitting it with his shoulder like a running back hitting a tackle bag.

Over three-hundred-pounds-of-angry struck the wall like an artillery shell, smashing through the bricks and barreling into the next room, roaring incoherently at the top of his voice.

Muller followed, bringing his shotgun to bear on the only occupant in the room. A man of late middle age, dark hand crafted suit, slicked back salt and pepper hair, douchebag pencil moustache, eyes like black pebbles and a set of long and very obvious fangs protruding past his obscenely red lips. On his hip, a sheathed rapier.

'Goodness me,' he said. 'How very impressive. That, I did not expect.'

'Not surprising,' said Tag. 'No one expects the Tag-man to come through their bedroom wall.'

The vampire chuckled. 'Very true, young man.' Then he pulled out a gold-plated Colt 45 and shot Tag in the chest. Twice.

'Don't do that,' yelled Tag. 'I got no spare shirts

left.'

The vampire shot him again and raised an eyebrow in astonishment. 'My, this is a day full of surprises,' he said. 'What are you?'

'I'm not a what,' replied Tag. 'I'm a who. Tag be my name; you blood sucking fiend.'

Now, that is just rude,' responded the vampire. 'And who might you be?' he asked Muller.

'I might be Bugs Bunny,' replied Muller. 'But I'm not. I'm actually sergeant Dietz Muller, Knight of the Holy See.'

'Muller the Pious,' breathed the vampire. 'That is unfortunate.'

'For who?' asked Muller.

'Well, for me, of course. Your reputation precedes you. I may be old and powerful, but I am no fool. Many have attempted to stand against you. None have succeeded. Looks like my run has come to an end. However, I hope you don't mind, but I shall not go gentle into that good night. I shall fight.' He drew his rapier.

But before the vampire could do anything, Tag drew both Eagles and opened up, hitting him with six .50 caliber, silver jacketed rounds. All six struck him in his right temple, expanded to almost a full inch in diameter and exited via his left temple, taking most of the contents of his skull and the entire left side of his head with them.

Then Muller stepped forward and, with a single swing of his sword, he decapitated the demon.

Both hunters stared at the body for a few seconds.

'That was a little anticlimactic,' said Muller.

'Yeah,' agreed Tag. 'And now I ain't got no shirts.'

Muller chuckled at his friend's discomfort.

'You know,' mused Tag. 'This is the first ancient we've found in Italy for a while. I must admit, I thought we had killed them all after the last great battle. Let's face it, the Italian and British branches of the *Nosferatu* were all but extinguished.'

Muller nodded. 'I agree. But this vampire, he wasn't Italian.'

'How do you know?' asked Tag. 'After all, when they're that old they don't have any real discerning accent as such.'

Muller shook his head. 'Not true. Most retain some semblance of their original dialect. Or at least they talk in such a way that favors their favorite area of abode.'

'This bloodsucker sounded like an upper-class Brit,' said Tag.

Again, Muller shook his head. 'No,' he said. 'He talked like someone who wanted to sound like an upper-class Brit. Think of Sir William, that is what a true British noble sounds like, and he sounded nothing like this idiot. This ancient was more Dick Van Dyke than Prince William.'

'What you saying, mister Knight?'

'I'm not sure. But I think we should investigate this house a little before we go. See if we can get any more leads on this vampire's background. There's something going on here and I don't like it. Not at all.'

CHAPTER 8

Father Dubois gave up. He had been pedaling as fast as he could in an attempt to follow Troywolf and Emily. But it was to no avail. They ran faster than a motorbike. Faster than a racing car.

And at the same time, Troy had his nose to the ground, following a trail of scent.

The priest took a handkerchief from his pocket and mopped the sweat from his face. If he was honest with himself, he was actually relieved he was unable to keep up with the beautiful blonde and the huge werewolf.

He knew they were on his side, a Knight of the Holy See had assured him, but that didn't mean the two strange people – creatures? – did not cause him undue stress. Fear even.

For it was difficult to be in the presence of such raw power and not feel utterly, helplessly intimidated.

Troywolf kept running. The trail was strong, the stench of vampire easy to track. And next to him, Emily ran – her movements smooth and effortless. She carried Troy's clothes in a small rucksack, along with her cell phone, some water and a pack of beef jerky. No weapons.

After many months, they were hunting again.

And the enemy would tremble with their coming.

Em was quite capable of going wolf if she needed to, having absorbed the ability after crossing over to the river Styx with a deceased pack alpha, and returning with Troy's help. As well as this, she was the world's only Daywalker. A vampire no longer constrained by either daylight or the need for human blood.

However, as gifted as she was, Troy was the Omega wolf. The Alpha of alphas. Leader of all of the werewolf packs. A position he had inherited from Sir William. This meant he had an ability that allowed him to morph into wolfman mode, a humanoid wolf creature, as well as a normal werewolf.

And, as Omega, his ability to track was beyond superlative. Even now, as they ran, he was using scent to track the vampire from the last murder. Despite the incident having occurred a couple of days prior, and the vampire had used a car to leave the scene.

This was a feat beyond Emily's capabilities.

They ran through back lanes and country roads. Past vineyards, small farms and the odd farmhouse. As always, Em marveled at the beauty of the structured landscape of the French wine region. Gentle hills covered with grape vines, green grass, oaks and chestnut trees. She could sense small packs of wild pigs, the odd deer, rabbits and various game birds.

Troywolf stopped, raised his head, growled softly and looked up at a house on a nearby hill. A three story, white, villa with a couple of towers, a high stone wall, sculpted gardens, nestled in amongst ancient grape vines. Not quite a grand Chateau, but very close. Perhaps the size of a decent boutique hotel. Most likely, twenty bedrooms, a ballroom, and a smattering of rooms for entertainment.

Troywolf morphed into his wolfman mode. Standing upright, almost eight feet tall. Muscles on top of more muscles, as though an impatient sculptor had packed them on using raw concrete as opposed to smoothly chiseling marble.

The wolfman had assumed his more humanoid form because he found it easier to verbally communicate that way. Even though it was possible for him and Emily to talk mentally, that was more via thoughts and feelings. Pack communication. Verbal was more human. A more accurate way to transfer complex decisions and details.

'He's up there,' growled Troy. 'In the fancy house. I can smell it from here. But he's not alone. There are others. Vampires. Humans, most likely familiars. Even grinders.'

'How many?' asked Emily.

'Many,' grunted Troy. 'I would have to get closer to give an accurate figure.'

Emily thought for a while. 'Right,' she said. 'Now, or should we wait until night?'

The wolfman shrugged. 'Easier to remain concealed at night. But then again, that is when the bloodsuckers are at their most vigilant. Six of one, half a dozen of the other. Your call.'

'We go tonight,' decided Emily. 'After all, we're simply scouting, quick in and out, see how many vamps there are, get a more accurate lay of the land. We can make a more informed decision after that.'

Troy nodded his agreement and the two of them found a shady spot to settle down until the night came.

CHAPTER 9

After they had recced the vampire's mansion, Emily and Troy had visited the site of the first victim. And although that had taken place almost two weeks before, it took Troy mere seconds to confirm that although it was a different combination of scents, there was a similar base note.

A group of at least three vamps, one of them being the same one that killed the second victim.

By then it was approaching midnight and they headed home.

'Okay,' said Em. 'From what we can tell, there's a master, at least four younger vampires, more than ten grinders and a similar number of familiars.

'And judging from the mix of scents you picked up, the elder is taking his brood out to feed,' said Emily. 'They must be fairly new. Still learning.'

'We can take them,' said Troy as he lit a cigarette. He knew Emily didn't like the cancer sticks, but all werewolves smoked. After all, dread disease didn't affect them. Drink, drugs,

Tobacco – not a problem. Lung cancer, liver problems and heart failure were for mortals.

Emily shrugged and took a sip of her wine. They were sitting in their kitchen, going over the info they had gathered just a couple of hours earlier.

'Probably,' she admitted. 'But there is a lot of them.'

'So?'

'So, what if you get hurt? Or worse. A master bites you and turns you. I'm fine, you can't turn the already turned. But if something happened to you.' She shook her head and her eyes shone with unshed tears.

Troy took a drag, exhaled, grimaced and sighed. He hated it when Emily insinuated she was a vampire. Technically, he had to admit, she was. But she didn't drink human blood and she could walk in the daylight. So, vampire? Not so much.

'I can take care of myself, Em. Is this because of the last battle?' he asked.

'What do you mean?'

'I mean, what happened before, all of the deaths, none of that was your fault. We were Pack, we fought, some of us died. But we won. We exterminated the UK and Italian branches of the *Nosferatu*. We have rested, now it's time to get back in the fight. It's what we do.'

'But did we win?' asked Emily.

'Yes,' affirmed Troy. 'Pack members died, true.

But some of us survived. None of the enemy did.'

'I don't know how you can just ignore it,' noted Emily. 'Not a day, not an hour goes by without me thinking about one of them. All of them. Our friends. Our family. I'm not sure I can go through anything like that again, Troy.'

'*Life is suffering. To suffer is to live,*' stated Troy, repeating the pack motto. 'I'm not being callous, Em. I haven't forgotten. I too think of them all the time. But they died doing what they were meant to do. As warriors. Soldiers of the light. And as such will I remember them. With joy, and love. Not with sorrow and regret. It is the only way to truly honor them.

'We must be strong. Remember – *The strength of the wolf is the pack. And the strength of the pack is the wolf.*'

'There is no longer any pack,' whispered Emily.

She was surprised to hear the Omega chuckle. 'There is always pack, my darling. We may be diminished, but we exist. The pack may be widespread, but as Omega, I feel them. If I called, they would come, wherever they are, whatever country. There is always pack.'

The Omega stubbed his cigarette out and was about to speak again when he stopped. 'Car coming.'

Emily nodded her agreement. 'This place is like Grand Central,' she quipped. 'No one visits for almost a year, and now it's party time.'

Troy laughed again. 'I'd hardly call two visits, party-time.'

Emily stuck her tongue out at him. 'You know what I mean.'

'Whoever they are,' said Troy. 'They're definitely heading this way. Let's go outside, see who they could be.'

Emily nodded, turned off the house lights and the two of them ghosted out of the front door, disappearing into the shadows. Waiting.

A small Fiat bounced up the driveway, riding hard on its obviously overloaded suspension. It pulled up in front of the house, a huge man squeezed out of the passenger side and stretched.

Emily screamed. 'Tag.'

The big man turned to face her, and his face split into a wide grin. 'Hey, baby girl,' he shouted. 'Long time no see.'

Emily ran up and threw her arms around him, tears of joy rolling down her cheeks.

CHAPTER 10

Emily sipped the cup of strong, super-sweet milky tea Tag brewed for her. At first, she'd hated the industrial strength, syrupy concoction the big man called tea. But after a while it became her favorite drink. And it was only fairly recently she discovered the Jamaican spiked every pot with a pinch of marijuana.

But she didn't care. Because she knew, the more Tag liked you, the sweeter he made your tea. And that picked up her spirits and reminded her that, aside from Troy of course, she had other people who loved her. People who put her above themselves.

What Emily didn't realize was the fact that every surviving Pack member felt the same way as Tag. All of them would lay down their lives for her without question.

But then none of them made tea like the big man.

'So, how come you wearing a jacket with no shirt?' Troy asked the Jamaican.

Tag scowled. 'Because the boss keeps letting vamps shoot me. Now I run outa shirts. And they weren't cheap.'

'They were free,' interjected Muller. 'Courtesy of the Vatican tailors.'

'Yeah, but that still don't mean they was cheap,' insisted Tag. 'They cost me in blood and pain and pain.'

'You said pain twice,' quipped Muller.

'Of course,' agreed Tag. 'That's because it was really, really painful. You try getting shot like a hundred times. It sucks.'

'Vampires suck,' said Troy.

Tag banged the table. 'That true, boy,' he yelled as he laughed out loud. 'That true. Now, baby girl, talk to Tag about your local vamps.'

So Em and Troy laid out what had happened so far.

'Well, now that you got reinforcements,' stated Tag. 'We all good to go. I say we tool up and go waste those blood suckers, ASAP.'

Troy grinned. 'I'm in, big man. No time like the present.'

Muller and Em looked at each other and rolled their eyes.

'It's like dealing with a pair of kindergarten children,' said Em.

Muller grinned. 'At least they're keen. And I suppose they're correct. If it's going to happen, it might as well happen as soon as possible. Before the monsters strike again.'

And Em couldn't argue with that logic.

CHAPTER 11

The next morning the sun rose on the four hunters. An explosion of pink and purple and blue, painting the sky like a child with an unlimited palette.

They scaled the wall surrounding the mansion with laughable ease, and now they stood in the shadows, planning their next step.

'I've always been in favor of just going in through the front door and shooting everyone who gets in the way,' whispered Tag.

'Simple is good,' added Muller. 'Less to go wrong.'

'I think we should split up,' interjected Troy. 'We can do more damage that way.'

'I agree,' concurred Emily. 'Troy and I will hit the back door, Tag, you and Muller go through the front. Clear room by room, meet in the entrance hall. Then together we take the next floor. Anyone you see is most likely the enemy, so don't hesitate to take them out. There may be innocent prisoners being kept for feeding, but they'll be locked up. So, we hit hard and fast. Ready?'

'Ready like Freddy,' answered Tag.

Troy and Muller simply nodded.

Em stood up and adjusted her weapons. Like Tag, she favored the Desert Eagle pistol. However, as her hands were a lot smaller, she plumped for the 357-magnum version instead of the massive 50 cal.

Emily also had the ability to call on her battleax – Death walker. Summoning it from another dimension where it always waited for her, ready to feast on the blood of the evil ones.

Muller had his usual shotgun and sword combination.

Tag sported a pair of Eagles plus a set of webbing with extra mags and half a dozen V40 mini hand grenades, each the size of a golf ball. The mini-frags were perfect for room clearing.

Troy stripped down and changed into his wolfman form. He carried no weapons because he was Omega. Which meant he was the ultimate weapon.

With a nod, Em and Troy sprinted around the back of the mansion. Tag and Muller counted off twenty seconds and Tag did his battering ram thing, smashing the front door off its hinges and barreling into the entrance hall.

A human guard stood at the bottom of the sweeping stairway. He was dressed in a black uniform and carried a Heckler and Koch sub machine gun. Before he could bring it to bear, Muller hit him with both barrels of his sawn-off, throwing him backwards onto the stairs.

'Go left,' he shouted at Tag. 'I'll go this way. As soon as you've cleared your area, sound off and come back here.'

Tag nodded and strode off, both pistols drawn and ready.

He walked past an open pair of double doors and peered inside. An empty ballroom, in the corner a raised platform with a grand piano. Dull lighting, heavy drapes. Vampire 101.

Further along, a closed door. He kicked it open. A large sitting room. Probably referred to as a withdrawing room or something equally as fancy-pants. Also, empty.

Another door. Another sitting room. Empty.

'Hell, how much sitting do these people need to do?' Tag muttered to himself as he kicked open another door.

A study. A bespectacled man sitting behind a large desk. In front of the man, a computer screen. He looked up and frowned. 'You are not to be allowed in here,' he said in a strong Eastern European accent. 'Not without the permission of the master.'

'No shit? You a vampire?'

'Does you have ever seen a vampire wearing the eyeglasses?'

'No.'

'That does answers your question very much,' continued the man as he massacred his English grammar. 'Now for to look, to be obvious, you are new. But security staff must stick to their posts, they do not ever to go to wandering around. The master will punish you. Last warning for you, now leave.'

'You Polish?' questioned the big man. 'You sound Polish. Or something like that.'

'Get out, you big idiot.'

Tag shot the familiar in the face and closed the door behind him. He heard the boom of Muller's shotgun from the opposite end of the house and he grinned. They were doing business.

The final room was a large old-fashioned kitchen. Wood fired stoves, butchers chopping blocks and large tables. Also, four humans.

A female in a chef's hat, holding a cleaver. Two men in some sort of striped uniform and another uniformed guard.

The chef reacted first, throwing her cleaver at the big man.

Tag dodged to one side and fired, starting with the armed guard and moving left to right.

Four shots, four bodies.

He turned and jogged back towards the entrance hall, shouting as he did so.

'Clear.'

Seconds after he arrived, Muller ran in. He had a few spots of blood on his face and the collar of his shirt. It wasn't his.

'A couple of guards and someone who looked like a chauffeur,' reported Muller.

'One guard, an accountant with a funny accent

and some cooks,' replied Tag. 'Should we start with the next floor?'

'No,' Muller shook his head. 'Em told us to wait here.'

As he answered they heard a scream of agony ring out from the other end of the building.

The side Troy and Emily were attacking.

CHAPTER 12

Troy followed as Emily ran to the back of the building. She had expected the back door to lead to the kitchen, as that was the usual layout on houses such as these. Instead, they found what appeared to be a residential wing. A long bungalow attached to the rear of the building; all the windows covered with the standard heavy drapes.

The two of them proceeded to the back door. It was locked. Emily opened it by simply grasping the handle and turning until the mechanism shattered. Then she pushed it open and they went in.

A long corridor. No lights. Five doors on the one side of the corridor, two on the opposite.

Troy sniffed. Gestured towards the five doors. 'Vampires,' he growled. 'Fairly new ones.' Then he nodded at the first of the two opposite doors, both of them were bound in steel reinforcing. 'Grinders in the first one. Lots of them. That one, humans. They smell terrified. Most likely food.'

'Looks like the prisoners and the grinder's doors are locked from the outside,' noted Emily, pointing out the massive padlocks on the two doors.

'So, we take the vamps out first,' suggested Troy.

Emily nodded. 'I doubt their doors are locked, let's try for quiet. A door each.'

Troy nodded and tried the first door. Then he shook his head. 'Locked from the inside.'

'Well, there goes quiet,' said Emily. 'Okay, let's go in hard and fast. On three. One, two,' she kicked open the first door while Troy smashed straight through his.

The room was pitch black, but Emily could see as if it were daylight. A young woman lay on a large double bed. She looked like she was in her early twenties. Emily could smell her fetid stench from across the room. A base note of rotting meat with a top note of acetone. The product of a protein-only diet combined with the fact they were undead.

Emily drew her two pistols and fired four times. Every shot struck the vamp in the center of her forehead. There was a reason Tag always shot people '*inna face*' as he put it. It was the only way to take a vamp down with any real chance of success.

Then she ran across the room, holstering her weapons as she did so and, with a mere thought, she summoned Deathwalker. A casual swing and the vampires head leaped across the room like someone had punted it.

Turning fast, she banished the ax, drew her pistols and ran to the next room.

She could hear Troy savaging his chosen target, the sound of breaking bones and tearing flesh plainly audible from the next room. Before Emily reached the next door, it slammed open and a young man blurred out, moving as fast as only a vampire or werewolf could.

Supremely confident in his speed, the young vamp launched himself at Emily.

But to the Daywalker it was as if she were being attacked in slow motion. Drawing her pistols, she had more than enough time to pull off two rounds, hitting him in the chest and halting his forward motion with a pair of silver coated, .357 expanding rounds travelling at over 1700 feet per second.

As the young bloodsucker crashed to a halt, Emily stepped forward and delivered a perfect spinning roundhouse kick, striking him immediately below his bullet wounds with enough force to shatter all of his ribs and his spine. He sailed across the corridor and struck the opposite wall, fracturing his skull as he did so.

Emily summoned her ax again and beheaded him.

She turned to the next door, but saw Troy was standing in the middle of the corridor, a severed head in his one paw.

'It's done,' he growled as he dropped the head. 'What now.'

'The grinders, said Emily, swinging her ax and hacking off the padlock.

As she did so, the door exploded open and a clutch of screaming, deformed and filthy Grinders sprinted out of the room, slavering and keening as they came.

Grinders were a foe worth taking seriously. They were the detritus left over when a master vampire tried to turn a human unsuccessfully. Only a small percentage of humans were successfully turned. Most died, a large percentage became Grinders, and only a few made it to full bloodsucker.

When they became Grinders, the process cooked their brains and deformed their bodies. But at the same time, it imparted outlandish strength, speed and healing abilities.

Emily fired off her remaining ammo, dropped the pistols and brought Deathwalker into play.

The double-bladed ax blurred into constant motion. A ballet of blood and dismemberment.

Troy, who had fought alongside Emily many times before, moved in concert with her, striking where she missed, covering her back and ripping into the dozen or so Grinders with controlled savagery.

The battle took place at such superhuman speeds that it lasted mere seconds. In that time, Troy and Emily had dispatched, with great prejudice, thirteen fully developed Grinders.

Troy checked out the remains and then relaxed, satisfied that there was no longer a threat.

Emily, however, kept swinging her ax. Dicing and slicing the already dismembered bodies. Blood sprayed and pieces of flesh flew around the corridor as she lost herself to the divine madness of battle. The berserk killing rage she was prone to enter since she had become the Day-walker.

Reveling in the death and dismemberment.

The ultimate killing machine.

'Emily,' growled the Omega. 'Stop.'

Emily turned to Troy, her eyes glowing with madness, her face split into a mirthless grin as the blood and gore dripped from her hair and body.

'Enough,' shouted Troy.

Slowly, the insanity drained from her. And her human side reasserted itself.

Troy stepped forward and took her in his arms, growling softly as he did so.

'Sorry,' whispered Emily. 'It's been so long, I forgot how to retain my control.'

'No worries,' said Troy. 'It's what we do. Now let's go find Tag and Muller and finish this.'

'What about the prisoners?' asked Emily.

'I reckon they're safer locked away for now,' said Troy. 'After we've killed the master, we'll come back for them. Maybe phone father Dubois to come and help.'

Emily nodded. 'Let's do it.'

CHAPTER 13

'Hey, baby girl,' said Tag. 'You okay? You get cut?'

Emily shook her head.

'She's fine,' interjected Troy. 'Just got a bit carried away. We ran into a crowd of grinders and Em introduced them to Deathwalker.'

'We heard the screams,' noted Muller. 'Looks like it's all clear on this floor, you ready to move on?'

Emily nodded along with the rest of them. But Tag could see she was upset. He knew she hated it when her dark side came to the fore. And although he was quite prepared to die for her, there was little he could do to help the internal battle she would have to fight for the rest of her living days.

Because, when Nathan Tremblay, the Shadowhunter traitor turned vampire, had bitten Emily, he had gifted her with greater power than ever, he had also cursed her by bathing her soul in darkness. If she had not been such an inherently good person, she would have already succumbed to the power of the dark, so powerful was its call.

So, it came to pass, the being that was mankind's most effective weapon against the dark, had the potential to also be evil's greatest ally.

Tag and Muller led the way up the stairs.

Two guards waited at the top, hidden behind a large pillar in the center of the landing. One of them fired his pistol and managed to hit Tag in the shoulder before a fusillade of shots from both of the hunters cut them down.

Tag cussed while he waited for his flesh to knit back together.

The floor was strangely designed. The one side of the landing was open plan, densely covered by indoor plants. Due to the lack of natural light, the plants were radically etiolated. Unhealthy and stringy. More post-apocalyptic nightmare than peaceful greenhouse resting place.

On the right-hand side, a single oversized door.

Tag was about to go full battering ram when Muller leaned over and tried the handle.

'It's not locked,' he said.

'On three,' said Tag.

He counted down and Tag and Muller burst into the room, followed closely by Troy and Emily.

They entered a single room. Huge. The entire right-hand side of the building.

It was a bedroom. A humongous bed graced the center of the room. Ridiculously large.

Maybe ten times the size of a normal double. Complete with four posts, swags, drapes and countless overstuffed pillows and cushions.

There was a dressing table, a smattering of occasional chairs and another batch of the oddly unhealthy pot plants.

In front of the bed stood a man. Long silver hair slicked back into a tight pony tail. Clean shaven. He wore a silk maroon smoking jacket, black velvet trousers and carpet slippers.

In his left hand he held a pipe. A Meerschaum, ala Sherlock Holmes.

'Nice pipe,' said Tag.

The man smiled, exposing his long, glittering canines. '*Merci*,' he replied. 'It is always pleasant to meet a connoisseur.'

And then a wave of coercion crashed over both Tag and Muller, driving them to their knees as any form of personal choice was taken from them by the vampire's powerful glamor.

It was immediately apparent that this was no normal vamp. The fact he could so casually nullify both Tag and a Knight of the Holy See, meant he must be more than a mere Master. Most likely an Elder. Or perhaps even an ancient, a vampire in excess of a thousand years old.

'How pitiful,' he sneered. 'A pair of humans dare to take me on. It would be laughable if it were not so insulting. Now,' he continued. 'Time to die...'

But before he could do anything, Emily

stepped forward, conjuring Deathwalker as she did so.

The vampire looked up and blanched, involuntarily taking two unsteady steps backwards as raw fear etched itself across his features.

'The Daywalker,' he croaked. Then he looked at Troy. 'And the Omega.' He dropped his pipe and held up his hands. 'Wait,' he shouted. 'This does not have to end badly. I have information. Important information. Spare me and I shall give it to you.'

Tag and Muller stood up, no longer held by the ancient's glamor.

Troy growled.

Emily smiled. 'You will tell me what I want, regardless of whether I let you live or not.'

And she unleashed the full might of her coercion.

The ancient was driven to his knees as a tsunami of mental power crashed over him. Unfortunately, the amount of power was so great it drove both Tag and Muller to the floor once again. But this time their ears and noses started bleeding; such was the strength of Emily's mind control.

'Mercy. I will talk. *S'il te plaît, arête,*' he croaked in French. 'Please stop.'

'Emily,' shouted Troy. 'Stop.'

'No! No mercy.'

Troy grabbed her by the shoulders and turned her to face Tag and Muller. Both of them writhing on the floor in agony.

Emily flinched and immediately dropped her glamor.

The hunters let out sighs of release, and the ancient, who had been the target of Emily's aggression, let out a low moan of relief.

'That's twice now,' yelled Tag. 'And it's your fault,' he said, pointing at the vampire. Swearing under his breath, the big man pulled out a pistol and shot the vamp in his left elbow. A painful wound but not at all debilitating. Particularly as an ancient will heal up almost instantly.

Muller raised an eyebrow. 'Feel better now?'

Tag nodded. 'Much. Thanks.' Then he turned to Emily. 'Tell you what, girly,' he said. 'What say Muller and I get out of the room while you question this butt hole? Then you can tell us what he said afterwards. That way you won't explode our eyes by mistake or something.'

Emily nodded, shamefaced at the blunder that had caused her friends such pain.

Troy stalked over to the vampire and grabbed him by his neck to ensure he didn't try to escape. Then with a head gesture he motioned for Tag and Muller to leave the room.

Emily banished Deathwalker, stood closer to the vamp and, once more, lashed out with her coercion.

It was time to see what he knew.

CHAPTER 14

The ancient vampire had obviously harbored a penchant for young girls. Every one of the human prisoners being kept for feeding were female, between the ages of sixteen and twenty.

There were nine of them. Some French, but mainly foreign tourists. Backpackers touring Europe. Looking for adventure.

Now they were mere shadows of themselves. Terrified and malnourished.

Father Dubois arrived in a minibus, together with two nuns from the local parish. The nuns loaded the girls into the transport to take them back to the residence attached to the church.

Emily took the priest's bank details and assured him that she would transfer a serious amount of money into his account. More than enough to purchase new clothes, feed them and repatriate those who needed help getting home. She would also transfer a lump sum large enough to ensure the girls would all get a good start in their future life.

The father had hesitated at such a gesture, but Emily assured him that money was no object.

After the prisoners had been taken care of, Tag and Muller searched the building for more information and then put it to flame.

The hunters watched it burn to the ground.

Then they went back to the farmhouse to discuss their next steps.

***

The kitchen table was covered in various printed pages, a couple of old-fashioned ledgers and a laptop.

All stuff the hunters had removed from the mansion before torching the place.

'I have information on two more nests,' stated Emily. 'Both in France. One near Lyon, the other closer to Paris. Large. Maybe thirty strong. We'll need to clear those out as soon as we can. Looks like the French *Nosferatu* is stepping up their game. Strange, they've been fairly quiet of late.'

'Agreed,' said Muller.

Tag picked up one of the ledgers. 'What's that weird writing?' he asked.

'Cyrillic,' answered Muller. 'Russian.'

'That's what that accent was,' noted Tag. 'I thought maybe Slovakian, or Portuguese, or Polish.'

'Those three accents don't sound at all the same,' said Muller.

Tag shrugged. 'Whatever. Foreign.'

'You're foreign,' pointed out Muller.

'No, I'm not,' denied Tag. 'I'm English Jamaican.'

'That's foreign to me,' quipped the Knight.

'Whatever. That speccy guy with the accent, he was the accountant,' said Tag. 'I think. Looked like an accountant.'

'Judging from this material, I agree. But that begs the question, what is a French ancient doing with a Russian accountant?' mused Muller.

'Outsourcing?' ventured Troy.

Muller shook his head. 'The Italian and British *Nosferatu* were very unusual in that they co-operated so closely. Normally, vampires are incredibly territorial. And none more so that the French and the Russians. To the point where I have never heard of a French vampire having a Russian familiar, or vice versa.'

'Times change,' said Emily.

'Not unless there is a reason,' countered Muller. 'It would be like Republicans and Democrats teaming up together.'

'That's happened before,' argued Emily. 'During the Second World War. The two parties decided to work together for the sake of winning the war.'

'Exactly,' said Muller. 'I fear a war may be coming. And if the vampires have decided to put aside their differences in order to take on humankind, may our Lord help us.'

CHAPTER 15

He had once befriended count Vlad the Impaler and Genghis Kahn. But they were mere children compared to his vast age.

The centuries had blended into millennia, and the millennia became an unending blur of mankind's repeated blunders. War after war, ignominy heaped on top of ignobility. Famine, mass starvation and disease, most of it brought about via political ineptness or simple greed.

Man's inhumanity to man.

And they dared to call him a monster.

But he was old. Perhaps the oldest being on the planet.

In fact, such was his age he had advanced to the stage where he had become almost ethereal. His physical being superfluous, close to non-existent. A ghostly apparition held together solely by his enormous powers built up over thousands of years.

And he had been the unchallenged *Tzar* of the entire Russian House of the *Nosferatu* for many hundreds of years.

The Ancient one had ruled from his *Dvorest*, or

Palace surrounded by over three hundred vampires, grinders and familiars. The magnificent dwelling situated on the shores of the Pripyat River.

Some twelve miles from Chernobyl.

His people knew him as the *Krov Tsar.* The Blood King, Aquilla Belikov. But he vaguely remembered a time before. When his name had been different. Aagha Erdogan. And before that, Angelo Alexopolous.

And even further back ... Gar. Just, Gar. He thought it may have meant Lion. Or leopard. But that was so long ago.

Before iron.

Before the wheel.

Before...

But after shoddy Soviet construction and communist disregard for safety procedures had caused the Chernobyl Nuclear Plant to melt down, and cover the entire area with approximately *four hundred* times more toxic radiation than was dropped on Hiroshima, things had changed.

Obviously, all of the familiars died. Some fast, most slowly. In great pain.

But the brethren could not die. Although, over the next few years, many of them wished they had.

Because while the radiation could not kill them, it did change them. For most of the survivors it took almost three years before they

69

fully adapted to the massive quantities of radiation poisoning.

By then *the change* had taken place.

Out of a clutch of one hundred and twenty Grinders, fifty Aspirants, twenty-six Masters and three Ancients – not including Belikov - only forty-one remained.

All the Grinders, and most of the Aspirants had met with the true death. Even their supernatural abilities to heal were not sufficient to fight off the radiation.

The survivors were no longer the suave, sophisticated creatures of physical beauty they had once been.

No.

The survivors were all now truly monsters, both in their inner selves and in the way they looked.

Hideously deformed with humped backs, extra-long canines, misshapen, lumpy features and gigantic slabs of muscle that would have looked out of place on the Hulk.

As well as the physical changes, their healing rates, strength and speed had more than doubled.

As had their need and desire for human blood.

However, unlike before, these new Uber-vampires could no longer blend in with society. Not for them picking hapless victims from a nightclub or off the street. They were simply too hideous to be seen without creating mass panic.

They either hunted under the cover of darkness, or they used familiars to collect their food for them.

And now, over thirty years after the Chernobyl meltdown, *Krov Tzar* Aquilla Belikov, Blood King, ancient and leader of the Russian *Nosferatu* was more powerful than he had ever been. With over a hundred familiars at the palace and more than two hundred working for him in various positions around the former Soviet Union, plus over a hundred recently turned Aspirants, he was ready to take the next step in what he saw as the Uber-vampire's evolution.

Two of the guards opened the doors to the throne room and bowed as his oldest friend and head of his enforcement branch walked in. Jebe Zurgadai.

Belikov had met him in 1206, when Jebe was one of Genghis Kahn's most trusted generals. After Genghis died, during a campaign in China, Belikov had turned Jebe, and together they had traveled across China to eastern Europe, to Kiev and then on to Hungary, where he befriended King Emeric.

However, after King Emeric died and his four-year-old son was crowned king, Belikov decided to move on.

And now, many centuries later, Jebe was still his most trusted advisor, instead of the Khan's.

'Some of the smaller houses are still resisting our advances, my *Tzar*,' informed Jebe after greeting his friend and master.

'Name them.'

'The Saratov's, the Volodga's and the Moldovan's.'

'Of course, the Moldovans,' sighed Belikov. 'Why does Count Lingu always have to be so contrary? Obviously, we need to bring them to heel. Our plans cannot proceed until all of the Russian houses are united. Under my banner, of course.'

'I think we should make an example of the Moldovans,' suggested Jebe.

'Lingu is a popular master,' stated Belikov. 'And he holds much sway with the other masters.'

'All the more reason we should attack him without mercy. We need to show anyone who sits on the fence that we will simply smash the fence out from underneath them. The time for negotiation has passed. Now is the time for blood and steel.

'And after we have united the Russian *Nosferatu*, we can begin the search for the *Triginta Argenteous.*'

The Blood King smiled, an expression of such horror and evil that even Jebe almost flinched.

'Yes,' breathed the king. 'The *Triginta.* The unholy artifact that will give me power over all of the *Nosferatu*.

'And then I shall become Blood King of the known world. *Krov Tzar* Aquilla Belikov. Emperor.'

CHAPTER 16

Belikov had tasked Jebe with the attack on the Moldovan house run by Count Lingu.

The Moldovan headquarters was situated in a twentieth century Soviet era apartment block next to a small ornamental lake in a town called Soracha. The exterior of the concrete building was a combination of austerity and solidity.

Around the building, a collection of residential bungalows, a market square and a town hall.

The entire town was controlled by the family, and everyone in it worked for them in some way. They were considered a small House, but a powerful one.

As discussed, Jebe was going in heavy handed.

Forty familiars, fifty Aspirants and ten masters.

The familiars were primarily to handle the artillery. Four 2B11 120 mm mortars, each with a crew of five, plus drivers and assistants. The familiars set the mortars up just over a third of a mile from the Moldovan HQ, stacking hundreds of rounds of HE and incendiary rounds ready to fire.

The vampires were ensconced in luxury people carriers. Darkened windows, aircon, satellite comms, and full entertainment systems.

Jebe had instructed the mortar crews to begin their bombardment six minutes before sundown. A trained 120mm mortar crew can maintain an extended rate of fire of ten rounds a minute. Six minutes gave them enough time to launch approximately three hundred rounds. Enough to flatten most of the small town of Soracha.

Then, as the sun went below the horizon, the vampires would attack, finding and exterminating any survivors. Even with advanced healing capabilities, it is extremely difficult to survive a direct, or even indirect hit from a round containing thirty pounds of high explosive.

Regardless of this, there would be survivors. There are always survivors after any bombardment, no matter how fierce, and *Tzar* Belikov's brethren were there to tear those survivors to shreds.

This was not meant to be war – it was a mass extermination.

The clocks counted down. And approximately six minutes before sunset, fire rained down from the skies. Hundreds of pounds of explosive followed by hundreds of incendiaries pummeled the town and then put it to flame.

Vampires huddled under whatever cover they could find, unable to venture out into the fast-waning sunlight, while human familiars and servants ran screaming in an attempt to escape the carnage.

At the six-minute mark the mortars stuttered to a halt as the sun retired.

Belikov's vampires descended.

Then the real butchery began.

The house of Moldovia fought back as well as they could. But after such a pounding, few were able to react as fast and as well as they normally could. And Jebe had insured he had brought only the most savage of his brood.

By midnight only the Blood King's brethren walked Moldovan soil.

The point had been made.

Resist the Blood King at your peril.

There could be only one master of the Russian *Nosferatu.*

Krov Tzar Aquilla Belikov.

CHAPTER 17

Muller used his contacts and Emily's access to funds to organize the team's transport.

A customized, six berth Globetrotter Motorhome. The major differences between the normal Globetrotter and Muller's one was the light armor plating and run-flat tires. Plus, the fact that two of the berths had been converted into an armory. The standard engine had also been replaced with a BMW five-liter V8, effectively doubling the horse power and adding fifty percent to the top speed. To ensure stability, the suspension had been both lowered and strengthened.

The plan was to proceed first to the nest in Lyon and then, after they had cleared that out, on to Corbavel near Paris.

Muller took the wheel while Troy and Emily sat in passenger section. Tag was busy inspecting the contents of the armory.

'Hey,' he shouted to Muller. 'Were did all this stuff come from?'

'Local representative of the Vatican. Why do you ask?'

'Man, there's enough firepower in here to start World War Three. Machine guns, 51mm light mortar, some sort of grenade launcher, pistols, hand grenades, loads of silver coated ammo, selection of rifles, sub machine guns, silvered knives. Oh, look, more Holy Water. Wait – shut the front door. Oh yes, baby come to Tag.'

'What?' asked Emily.

'Daddy got himself a replacement for Missus Jones,' answered the big man.

Emily rolled her eyes. Tag was referring to the Minigun he used to carry before he had gone touring with Muller. Em had no idea what had happened to the original Missus Jones but she was glad Tag had a replacement. Simple pleasures for a simple man.

She looked over and watched the big man stroke the M134 Minigun like it was a pet dog.

'What you going to call it?'

'She,' answered Tag. 'Not it. Anyway, her name is Missus Jones. They all called Missus Jones.'

The big man started to sing.

Me and Mrs. Jones
We got a thing, goin' on
We both know that it's wrong
But it's much too strong
To let it go now.

Troy chuckled. 'One of life's classic love affairs,' he quipped.

'It's a five-hour trip,' informed Muller. 'Estimated time of arrival, around three o'clock this afternoon.'

'Unless we stop for a nice lunch,' interjected Tag.

'Unless we stop to eat,' admitted the Knight. 'I've booked us into a bed and breakfast establishment close to our target. It's run by a trusted member of the church. I suggest we get there, and then get some transport more suited to scout out the vamps. A small saloon of some sort.'

There was a general mumble of agreement. Muller put the vehicle in gear and pulled off.

The next chapter of Emily's life had started. She was back in the game.

CHAPTER 18

Madame Dupont smiled broadly as she served the table a third helping of *cassoulet*. Never before had she met people with such healthy appetites. And such a love for her food. She had been warned to cook enough for a football team, and she had. Because when the church advised, you obeyed.

And when she saw only four people exit the vehicle her heart dropped. Because a French person abhors the waste of good food even more than they despise war.

But there would be no wastage. They ate like trenchermen. Especially the skinny blonde girl.

Madame affectionally pat the girl on the shoulder as she crossed the kitchen to put the huge casserole dish back on the stove. Little blondes who ate like trenchermen were high on the nations like-list.

And as for the men – *ooh la la!* Such men. Every one of them tall, handsome and built like stone outbuildings.

They all projected an animal sex appeal like a lighthouse shining its light across the ocean.

Beware, ships run aground here. And women. And even men.

She brushed a lock of gray hair out of her eyes. If only she were twenty years younger.

Of course, that would make her sixty. Well, okay, sixty-three, but who was counting?

'Hey, mama. *Excusez-moi, s'il vous plait.* Could I get some more bread? Another one of those long, skinny loaves.'

Madame grabbed a couple of *baguettes* from her bread bin and brought them over to Tag, handing them to him with a broad smile.

Tag winked at her as she walked off.

Madame Dupont blushed with pleasure. Yes, she still had it. *La!* Such men.

After they finished eating, the team gathered in the sitting room. Madame supplied cognac and cigars and then left them to their privacy.

'Good food,' noted Troy as he rolled his cigar around, ensuring it was perfectly lit.

Muller poured cognacs for all and then they sat. 'So,' he started. 'We're agreed, we attack at sunrise.'

Emily nodded. 'From this afternoons recce, it's obvious there is good security and a lot of guards. At least the vamps will be off their game during the sunlight hours. That should give us some sort of advantage.'

'Don't need any advantage,' interjected Tag. 'We got Missus Jones.' He turned to Troy. 'Go high.'

The two men high-fived.

'Yes,' they shouted in unison.

Emily smiled. 'Children. Okay, gentlemen, as soon as you've all finished your cigars, let's get our heads down. Make sure we're ready for tomorrow.'

They muttered their agreement.

CHAPTER 19

When people envisage France, they tend to think of the Eiffel Tower, Paris, vineyards and Michelin stars. But normally, not medieval castles. That remains the domain of England, Scotland and Wales.

However, there are approximately forty-five thousand castles, or *Chateau* in France. Many of them still habitable. And many of them of vast size.

In fact, the team of hunters were looking at one right now. Unlike the classic British castle, this was basically a fortified mansion. With pointed spires and scores of fluttering flags, the structure was more Disney than Braveheart. But it was still a substantial edifice with high walls and serious security measures.

'That section of wall,' said Emily. 'It's a blind spot. The trees, no windows facing that way. That's our point of ingress.'

'True,' agreed Muller. 'But how do we get over? It's got to be twenty feet high.'

'Troy and I will scale it,' answered Emily. 'Then we'll drop a rope down and pull you and

Tag up. Do the same thing to let you down the other side.'

'Works for me,' said Tag. 'You okay with my weight plus Missus Jones. With extra ammo, the battery pack and my usual kit, it's an extra three hundred pounds. Add that to my weight, you looking at over six hundred pounds. That's over a quarter of a ton.'

Emily raised an eyebrow but didn't deign to answer what she considered to be a superfluous question.

'Come on,' she said. 'Let's get into position.'

The team thread their way through the surrounding vineyard, keeping to the long shadows cast by the rising sun, using their skills to remain unseen. They approached the wall with caution and, as they got there, Troy stripped down and changed into his wolfman form. Emily folded his clothes and stored them in one of the packs on her webbing.

Then she scaled the wall. There was no hesitation or seeking handholds. She simply crawled up the sheer face, digging her extended talons into the stone itself when she needed to. Troy followed, using his paws and supernatural strength to do the same thing.

As soon as Emily got to the top of the wall, she dropped the rope down, moving as fast as she could. Troy leaped from the top, into the grounds, and hid in the shadows at the base of the twenty-foot-high wall, keeping a lookout for any guards.

Muller tied the end of the rope around his waist and gave Emily a thumbs up. She pulled the knight up with ease, hauling him to the top of the wall and then easing him over and down into the Chateau grounds.

Then she dropped the rope for Tag. The big man connected himself up and Emily hauled. Getting the big man up and over was more of a challenge but the Daywalker still accomplished it with relative ease, dropping into the grounds herself as soon as Tag touched down.

They moved again, using the ornate shrubs, trees and verdant flower beds to remain concealed.

Emily was impressed at how much Tag had improved his skills since she had last seen him. He had always been game, but now she could see he had a gloss of professionalism he didn't have before. The year spent with a Knight of the Holy See had definitely upped his game. Despite the fact he was carrying almost three hundred pounds of ordnance he moved with a measured grace and stealth, as opposed to his usual Buffalo-ploughing-through-beach-sand mode of locomotion.

Muller showed his usual consummate professionalism as he covered ground.

As for the wolfman and the Daywalker – their ability to stalk was unprecedented. Even in the full morning sun they were almost impossible to spot.

The team were aiming for a side entrance. A door that seemed to be little used. Their objective, to get inside without alerting the sentries.

As they approached the door, Troy held his hand up, signaling them to stop.

A pair of huge Rottweilers came sprinting around the corner, lips pulled back exposing their canines, supremely confident in their ability to take on any comers.

They took one look at the wolfman and fell on their backs, exposing the bellies in a sign of complete and utter submission.

The team ignored them as they gathered outside the door.

Emily checked if it was locked, and when she found it was, she used her standard method of gaining access. Simply turning the handle until her strength defeated the mechanics of the lock.

Pushing the door open, she ghosted in, followed by the other hunters. They appeared to be in some sort boot-room. Perhaps a service entrance for staff during the rainy season. There were racks for wellington boots, scrapers to get mud off footwear and a wet area to wash off any dirt before it was tracked into the chateau.

Tag frowned.

'What's the problem, big guy?' asked Emily.

'A room for footwear,' he replied. 'It's obscene. When I was a kiddie, my whole family lived in a place the size of this room. Man, the rich are different.'

'I'm rich,' noted Emily.

Tag shook his head. 'No. You just got money. There's a difference.'

Emily grinned. The big man's simplistic views on life were refreshing. 'What say we go and kill a few of these rich folk,' she suggested.

Tag patted Missus Jones. 'We ready,' he affirmed.

Emily led the way.

They entered a long, dimly lit corridor. The walls were painted an institutional green. Gloss paint. The floors covered in 1970's linoleum. For some reason, the place smelled of boiled cabbage.

They were obviously in the servant's section of the chateau.

'Keep going,' advised Muller. 'Most likely, the kitchen and the servant's quarters will be close. I doubt we will run into any vampires in this part of the house. Maybe Grinders, although they are usually locked up, so most likely just familiars.'

'Whoever we come across, take them down quietly,' stressed Emily.

They all nodded, and Muller drew a pair of throwing knives from his webbing.

One of the doors on the side of the corridor opened. Troy reacted instantly, grabbing the person and smashing their head against the wall. They dropped soundlessly to the floor; their body utterly limp. Devoid of life.

Muller looked down at the body. A middle-aged woman. Dressed in a maid's outfit. His expression was disapproving, but he said nothing.

Emily took note and put her hand on the Knight's shoulder. 'Familiars are the enemy,' she said. 'This is total war.'

Muller nodded. 'I know,' he said sadly. 'And I will not hesitate to do the same. I merely wish I did not have to do so.'

They proceeded down the corridor, opening all of the doors as they did. Checking. Most of the rooms were bedrooms, except for a large janitor's closet, full of cleaning utensils, clothes and chemicals.

Three of the bedrooms were occupied, the servants having returned from what was obviously the night shift. After all, vampires tended to be more active at night.

Troy dispatched two of them and Muller killed the last one, a young man who reacted faster than the others, drawing a pistol as they entered the room. But before he could get a shot off, one of Muller's throwing knives sprouted from his throat, severing his jugular and halting his ability to shout a warning.

The Knight retrieved his blade, cleaned it on the fallen man's shirt and kept it ready for the next encounter.

At the end of the corridor, the last door did indeed lead to the kitchen. The team entered to discover ten people seated around a table, eating, plus a cook and two assistants standing at the stove.

A collection of servants returning from their night shift, and others breaking their fast before beginning a day's work.

Troy blurred into motion, attacking the cook and the assistants.

Muller's blades flashed through the air as he targeted the people at the far end of the table and Emily called forth Deathwalker.

It was a simple massacre. Most of the seated servants never even managed to stand before they were savagely chopped down.

Troy destroyed the cook and assistants, and Tag scragged the only man who did manage to get out of his seat, breaking his neck with a swift wrench.

Afterwards, the team avoided each other's eyes. They knew the fallen were all in league with evil. They knew that a familiar is merely the left hand of a vampire. And they knew that all familiars had to be destroyed.

But such wanton savagery did not sit well with any of them.

Except, perhaps, Emily. But that was not her true nature, it was merely her dark side striving for ascendance.

'Come on,' growled Troy. 'Upwards and onwards. We have a job to do. Let's so it.'

Once again, Emily led the way.

CHAPTER 20

'This place is a maze,' said Tag. 'You sure we going the right way?'

'This nose never lies,' growled Troy as he stalked down another seemingly endless corridor.

They were searching for the wing that housed the aspirants. If the house adhered to the customary *Nosferatu* norms, the Aspirant's rooms would be situated together, as they would still be spending time asleep during the day. As well as the fact that vampires were extremely conscious of one's levels and standings. Masters did not mix with Aspirants, although they did mix with Adepts on occasion.

Grinders would be kept somewhere else, as they were classed as little more than animals.

The team moved with great stealth, knowing that, although the Aspirants were most likely abed, the Adepts and Masters would be up, as they were at the level where they no longer really needed any sleep. And they could come across them at any moment.

Whenever they passed a window, Muller

would tear down the rubber backed drapes, letting the sun flood in. Turning the room into a vampire death trap.

He called it, combat decorating.

They came across a single familiar as they entered yet another dark corridor. The man was busy sweeping the carpets. Troy, who was still leading the way, dispatched him with a single punch that smashed him into the wall, crushing his skull and breaking his back as he did.

Then the wolfman stopped, sniffed the air and nodded.

'This is the corridor,' he announced. 'These doors.'

'Remember,' added Emily. 'We're still quiet. No guns if we can help it. Let's go two to a room. Troy and I. Tag and Muller. Take the occupant out, move on. We'll take the right side of the corridor; you guys take the left.'

'And don't forget to rip the drapes down to let the sun in,' said Muller. 'Give the vamps less places to hide if things go wrong. Oh, and Tag, no human battering ram, if the doors are locked, open them like Emily. Quietly.'

Tag frowned. 'No guns, no battering ram. You taking away Tag's best tools, man. Stripping the fun outa the whole game.'

The two teams took a door each, counted down and entered at the same time.

They worked fast and efficiently. This wasn't a duel; this was pest control. As Emily and

Troy entered their first room, Emily brought forth Deathwalker and decapitated the sleeping bloodsucker without hesitation or preamble. Troy pulled the drapes down and they moved on to the next room.

On the opposite side of the corridor, Muller's sword swung and Tag's massive Bowie knife stabbed as they exterminated the evil ones with cold efficiency.

Together, they managed to exterminate twelve Aspirants before Tag opened a door to discover one of the vampires awake. The bloodsucker reacted with their usual speed, blurring across the room to latch onto Tag's neck. With a savage yank, he ripped the big man's jugular open and then he leaped back, readying himself to take on Muller.

The Knight held his sword towards the vamp, weaving the point from side to side, covering himself. Then, as the creature was about to spring, Tag stood up, his neck healed.

The vamp hesitated for a split second as he stared at the big man.

'But, how?' it stammered.

Instead of answering, Tag used an overarm strike to slam his Bowie into the top of the vamp's head, striking so hard the blade buried itself to the hilt. Then he jerked the twelve-inch blade savagely back and forth until the vamp's brains were thoroughly scrambled.

Finally, he ripped it out and kicked the body

towards Muller who decapitated it with a casual backhand of his sword.

Fortunately, that was the only vamp awake and the rest were dispatched without further ado.

'Nice work, guys,' said Emily. 'Upwards and onwards, let's move, places to go, vampires to kill.'

The team followed her through a set of double doors at the end of the corridor, and then Troy took point, leading with his nose once again.

CHAPTER 21

There were seven houses present, gathered together in the vast ballroom of the Blood King's palace.

But even that huge space was not large enough to hold every member of every house present. So Jebe had limited the ballroom to Ancients, Masters and Adepts.

The Aspirants were delegated to a separate adjacent room.

There were over a hundred in the ballroom. Then the Aspirants bumped the figure up by another two hundred.

Over three hundred immortal creatures of power.

The world had not seen such a gathering since the time of King Arthur, when he fought the great war against the combined houses of the United Kingdom and Italy. It truly was an awe-inspiring sight.

And all waited for the appearance of the new self-proclaimed leader of all of the *Nosferatu* houses of Russia.

The *Krov Tsar.* Blood King, Aquilla Belikov.

The atmosphere was tense. It was obvious that some of the houses were here under pressure. Or because they had seen what happened to the house of Moldovia. But there was one thing all of the masters of the various houses agreed on. Belikov and his monstrously deformed and enhanced brood were creatures worthy of, if not respect, then fear.

It takes a lot to instill fear in a Master Vampire, but the Blood King had done it.

A frisson of excitement rippled through the gathering as the doors opened and Belikov strode in, surrounded by his honor guard. Ten humped backed, massively over-muscled monster vampires surrounding a warped and hideously deformed master.

'Kneel before your king,' demanded Jebe as he cast his gaze over the congregation.

With various degrees of hesitation, the gathering fell to their knees, heads bowed in a sign of respectful fear.

Except for the head of house Kiev. An ancient who was most likely the only vampire present who may have approached Belikov's vast age.

The Blood King stopped and stared at the ancient. 'Count Goncherov,' he greeted the ancient. 'You deem yourself too worthy to kneel before your betters?'

'You are not my better,' answered Goncherov. 'This assumption of leadership is not the *Nosferatu* way,' he continued. 'Our strength lies in our diversity. The fact that each house exists separately. Controlling its own businesses, hunting for its own food, disciplining its own members. Separate development together.'

Jebe started to move towards the Count, but Belikov stopped him with a gesture. Instead, he himself stepped out of his circle of guards and walked across to the recalcitrant Ancient.

The Blood King stood in front of Goncherov and smiled. A grotesque expression that was at odds with his lumpen, deformed features,

'How long have we known each other?' Belikov asked.

'I'm not sure,' answered the Count. 'Six, maybe seven hundred years.'

'And are we friends?'

Goncherov thought before he answered, and then he nodded. 'Yes. I think so.'

Belikov's dreadful smiled widened, exposing rows of shark-like teeth while a forked purple tongue lashed across his swollen, livery lips. 'Oh, my good Count,' he continued. 'You are incorrect. You are no friend of the Blood King. You are nothing. Not even an inconvenience. Barely worth a thought. And you dare to challenge me?'

Goncherov saw the rest of the brethren around him stepping back. They were not even being subtle about it. Distancing themselves from the dead-vamp-walking. And he realized he had made a grievous error.

But it was too late.

Belikov's maw opened impossibly wide, un-hinging like a snake, and he struck, latching onto Goncherov's face and shaking him, tearing into his flesh and shattering his bones. Then, with a final savage twist, he tore the whole front of the Count's face off and spat it onto the floor.

He stepped back; his visage once again split by the insane grin, blood dripping off his chin.

'Finish him,' he commanded of his honor guard.

The members of the guard fell on Goncherov like a pack of ravening hounds, tearing him limb from limb, slicing and dicing his flesh and pulping his bones. Finally, when what remained of the Count was recognizable only as something that was once flesh, the Blood King ordered them to stop.

His gaze swept the room. 'Anyone else with a comment?'

The silence was deafening.

'Fine, now, let me tell you what we are going to do. From this moment on, every member of every house under my rule will obey without question. Do you understand?'

There was a muted chorus of agreement.

'Do you understand?' repeated the Tsar.

This time, the reply was much louder. Some even stamped their feet in approval, or clapped loudly in support.

'Better,' said the King. 'This, my beloved brethren, is just the beginning. Look around you and mark who stands by your side. Because in the centuries to come you will be able to tell your sires, I was there. At the very start, when the Blood King set the *Nosferatu* on their ordained path.

'When King Belikov set *the prophecy* in motion.

'I was there when he declared that the *Nosferatu* would rule the world.'

There was a stunned silence – then in singles, and finally as a group, they began to cheer.

Krov Tsar.

Krov Tsar!

KROV TSAR!

CHAPTER 22

Marie Petit had survived the French revolution. Her family, however, had all ended up with their heads in a basket at the end of the guillotine.

The same night her family all perished, she gained eternal life. Or at least, eternal un-death. Her master and sire was a French revolutionary by the name of Jacques Cordelia, a close friend of both Robespierre and Georges Danton, the leaders of the revolution.

Unbeknown to most, Cordelia was the actual driving force behind the revolution. The leaders thought that he only met at night or in cellars due to his need for secrecy, never once suspecting he was an ancient vampire.

And the fact that the revolution resulted in the deaths of over forty thousand people and caused the streets of France to run red with blood, amused the Master vampire no end.

Even his turning of Marie instead of sending her to the guillotine was purely due to his twisted sense of humor. He looked to create chaos and reveled in the resulting anarchy.

Cordelia was dispatched soon after the revolution, by a Polish nobleman and hunter known only as, Von Helwing. The noble later acquired a certain amount of fame when he was cast as a vampire hunter in Bram Stoker's Dracula, wherein Stoker mistakenly called him, Van Helsing.

And now, Marie Petit was the leader of her own small house. She had re-purchased her family chateau and treated her servants and subjects just as she had before the revolution.

Vive la révolution

Let them eat cake.

Or blood, as the case may be.

Marie was the Master. There were no mistresses in the *Nosferatu*. Misogyny and chauvinism did not exist. Personal power was all that mattered. And Marie was exceptionally powerful.

At the moment, she sat at the head of a large dining table. It was one of her notable foibles that she insisted on feeding at a table. Having the victims served up as if they were part of a banquet.

Twenty vampires sat opposite her. Three Masters and seventeen Adepts. There were a further nineteen Aspirants in her house, but all of them were recently turned and spent most of the daylight hours sleeping, or at least resting.

The brethren were waiting for the familiars to bring their food.

Tonight's repast consisted of a clutch of teenagers Marie's household manager had purchased from a new supplier. Although Marie encouraged hunting for food, she insisted that the members of her house did not overhunt the local area. They were allowed the odd home grown treat, but on the whole they were instructed to travel at least six hours from the chateau to hunt. As a result, she often ordered food in.

She had a system of traffickers who supplied fresh young humans from places as far afield as Vietnam and Africa. After all, variety is the spice of life.

Lately, a large percentage of her supplies were being provided by a new player on the market. A Russian named Pytor Smirnov. Dealer in humanity.

And talking about food, it wouldn't do to show, but Marie was less than impressed with the service her familiars were delivering this morning. When she sat down at the head of the table, it was customary for the food to arrive *poste haste*.

She would be sure to discipline the serving staff and the wranglers for this oversight, although, in front of her brethren, she would not let her ire show. To show emotion showed weakness. And the weak did not last long as the head of a house.

Regardless, though, this sort of service was unacceptable. She was about to command one of her subjects to go see where the servants were, when she noticed the door opening.

'About time,' she murmured to herself.

And then the world around her turned to fire.

CHAPTER 23

Troy stood outside the door and nodded. 'They're in here,' he whispered. 'At least twenty of them. They smell like they're all high level. Masters and Adepts.'

Emily turned to Tag. 'What say we open the door and then you and Missus Jones introduce yourselves?'

Tag grinned. 'We all ready. It's date night for me and Missus Jones.'

'Wait,' interjected Muller as he took a brace of grenades from his webbing. 'These grenades have silver shot in them. Why don't I throw these in first, as they explode, Tag does his thing?'

Emily gave the Knight a thumb up. 'Go for it. I'll open the door, you guys go for it, and as soon as Missus Jones stops talking, we go in hard.'

Emily opened the door, Muller chucked the grenades in. Two seconds later they exploded and the big man entered the room.

The General Electric M134 Minigun fires a 7.62 round at a rate of approximately 6000 per minute. This works out to 100 rounds a second.

Tag was carrying 1000 rounds of ammunition. He expended the entire stock in just over ten seconds.

But the vampire is an incredibly hardy creature, and although the grenades and the gatling gun had torn many of them to shreds, there were still a few in combat condition.

But not for long.

Troy and Emily bound into the room, axe swinging, claws tearing and teeth crunching.

Muller followed, his silver throwing knives blurring across the room as he threw them at the remaining vamps.

Tag dropped Missus Jones and drew his twin Desert Eagles, adding his .50 cal rounds to the general pandemonium.

The room descended into utter chaos as blades and fire filled the air.

Twenty seconds later, the only vampire left standing was Marie, master of house Petit. Almost unbelievably, she had managed to remain unscathed through the entire massacre.

She stared at the hunters with raw, undisguised hatred. Then she threw herself at them

Emily called up Deathwalker and stepped forward, blocking her attack.

The rest of the hunters stepped back as the two women went at each other. The Master vampire and the Daywalker.

It was almost impossible to follow the combat, such was the speed at which it was being fought. Bodies blurred back and forth across the room, disintegrating furniture, smashing into walls and throwing kicks and punches at literal sound-breaking speed.

After twenty seconds it started to slow down as each took measure of one another, and the fight became less a display of speed and strength and more a test of skill.

The two circled each other, lashing out every few seconds, parrying, kicking and moving.

But after another half a minute it became blatantly apparent that Emily was merely playing with the Master.

Marie stopped moving, dropped her guard and shook her head. 'You treat me with so little respect,' she said. 'Am I not even worth your full effort? You will not do me the small honor of fighting me as an equal? Rather, you play with me like a cat with a bird. Why? Do you seek to humiliate me?'

Emily scoffed at the bloodsucker. 'You aren't worthy of respect,' she said. 'You're simply an evil leach. Lower than the lowest insect. And I play with you like a cat with a *rat*, not a bird.'

Marie shrieked in anger and launched herself at the Daywalker.

Emily met her charge with a spinning back roundhouse kick that landed with such ferocity it propelled the vampire across the room and smashed her into the opposite wall with enough force to shatter every bone in her body.

Emily sneered in absolute disgust. 'Muller,' she said. 'Finish it.'

The Knight of the Holy See walked up to the prostrate Master vampire and drew a flask of Holy Water from his webbing.

'The power of Christ compels me.'

CHAPTER 24

Father Monet was there at Muller's request. He was a short, rotund man who wore a threadbare, faded cassock that was once black and was now a dirty brown. It was also at least two sizes too small for him and stretched uncomfortably across his ample belly.

He stood next to Tag, his diminutive stature making him look a bit like a volleyball next to an oak. Together they watched the chateau burn.

Earlier, after the team had dispatched Marie, they had proceeded to the basement where the Grinders were held. A few grenades and a couple of homemade Molotov cocktails later and the Grinders were no more.

A quick search later, and they had led the human prisoners from the building.

After Emily questioned had them, and she gotten a name.

A Russian. Pytor Smirnov.

She also got an address to one of his warehouses near the city of Nice.

There were twenty-two souls. Again, mostly

young, late teens to early twenties. Various nationalities.

As before, Muller had used his contacts in the church to provide succor and shelter for the victims. And once again, Emily made funds available to ensure their transition back into society was made as easy as possible.

'They scare me,' said father Monet softly, as the flames consumed the mansion.

'Who? Vampires?' asked Tag

The priest shook his head. 'Them,' he pointed at Muller. 'The Knights of the Holy See. Particularly that one. Muller the Pious.'

Tag chuckled. 'Why?'

'His holiness shames me. The rock upon which his faith is built. He suffers not from vacillation or hesitance. He is resolute. Strong. The strength of his belief belittles my weak attempts.'

Tag shook his head. 'Oh, church-man, you got it all wrong. Trust me. It's easy to have faith when you do what we do. When you bang up against proper evil day in and day out, it's easy to maintain your faith.

'But what *you* do, dealing with reality. Helping people with their proper lives, their daily worries. That takes serious faith.

'What I'm saying is, it's easy to know the devil exists when you see him every day. But if you've never seen him, then it's a lot harder. It takes faith like yours to keep fighting the good fight. What we do, what Muller does, it's simple. Black and white. We don't have to sift between the grays. We see, we kill. You see, you help. You save,

'Father, take it from me – you da man.'

Father Monet didn't reply. But when Tag looked at him, he noticed the man's eyes glistened with unshed tears.

'Thank you, my son,' he said, eventually.

'No worries, church-man,' replied the Jamaican. 'You keep doing what you doing. Now, we gotta go, you okay with this?'

Monet nodded.

Tag followed the rest of the team to their transport. It was time to plan their next step.

It was time to visit Pytor Smirnov, put a stop to his business and find out what yet another Russian was doing involved with the French *Nosferatu*.

CHAPTER 25

'I'm sure we could force at least some of the smaller European houses to gather under our banner,' said Jebe. 'After all, we have been seeding our people amongst them for a while now. Accountants, familiars. I have even commanded Pytor to begin supplying food to some of the French and German houses.'

'Yes, you have done well, my friend,' said Belikov. 'But such is the nature of the true *Nosferatu* that they will never bend a knee to a foreign house. They barely cooperate amongst themselves. And for my plan of total domination to come to fruition, I must demand more than mere allegiance. I must have total subservience. I need them to submit utterly.'

'But still...' started Jebe.

'No. There is no but. We both know the only way to make this work is to find the *Triginta Argenteous*. The artifact that all *Nosferatu* must bow before. Once I have that in my hands, I will have total control over all of the brethren.'

Jebe did not answer, but his expression of disbelief showed through his lumpen, deformed features.

Belikov laughed, an ugly grating sound. 'I see you still harbor doubt,' he said.

Jebe bowed his head, but he did not gainsay the Blood King.

'Speak, Jebe,' insisted Belikov. 'We have been together for almost a thousand years. You have nothing to fear from me. What is the problem?'

'I mean no disrespect, my *Tsar*,' answered the ancient. 'But the *Triginta?* Obviously, I have heard the stories, the power the artifact holds over all. The prophecy is known to all who are *Nosferatu*.

'And lo, when the man of Kerioth be turned, his bane shall carry the authority of the disciples. And upon his true death will the Triginta Argenteous *hold that power in perpetuity until it be released by its holder.*

'But is that not merely myth and legend?'

'You have the prophecy down word for word,' acknowledged Belikov. 'But as you say, it is mere meaningless gobbledygook if you know not what it pertains to.'

'Forgive me, *Krov Tsar*,' said Jebe, head held low in respect. 'My ignorance shames me. Enlighten me, my king.'

'Do you at least know who the man of Kerioth is?' asked Belikov.

Jebe shook his head.

'I see. We have been together so long but there are still times when I forget you are a stripling compared to me. How old are you now?'

'Eight hundred and seven years, my king.'

Belikov chuckled. 'I remember when man was just beginning to forge iron. So many thousands of years ago the memories are now all but mists in my mind. However, be that as it may – Kerioth was the birth place of one, Judah Lebbaeus.'

Jebe looked blank.

'You will likely know him by his other name. Judas Iscariot,' prompted Belikov. 'The great betrayer. What few know about Iscariot is that, contrary to popular belief, he did not hang himself. No, instead he was actually turned by an ancient Master called, Augustus Sextus. An ex-*Tribunus* in the Roman army.

'Iscariot never joined a house, instead he roamed the earth as a lone vampire. Cursed and despised by all. Not only as the great betrayer, but also as *Nosferatu*. Eventually he was killed in a meaningless scuffle on the borders of Germania some five hundred years later.

'The Visigoth king, Euric, who was still a mere chieftain at the time, was involved in the scuffle. After the fight, he looted Iscariot's body.

'And on it he found the thirty pieces of silver that Judas accepted from the Romans in return for betraying his Lord and friend.

'After all those years, he never spent it, nor let it leave his side.

'Euric had no idea what the silver was, but he was fascinated by the coinage, noting the date and seeing how old it was. As well as this, he sensed a great power emanating from the coins. An almost physical presence, as if they were speaking to him, cajoling him, promising him.

'So, he kept the silver for himself, setting the coins in a necklace to wear at all times. It became a symbol of his office.

'But what Euric did not know, is the coins were cursed, and blessed at the same time. They had been blessed with the power of the disciples, in as much they inspired great loyalty amongst any whom the wearer would have follow them. Fanatical loyalty. Devotion without question or choice. In other words, if the wearer demanded obsequiousness, the subject was unable to refuse. They would become veritable disciples of the wearer. Such was the power of the coins.

'The problem was, at the same time, the silver was cursed. Because with the power of subservience came sure death. The wielder was cursed to die within years, if not months. The curse of the great betrayer.

'Thus, it came to pass that Euric became King and went on to be the only man ever to unite the Visgoth hordes. He managed to crush the Romans, and continued his advance until he controlled most of Europe.

'But then the curse struck, and after a mere twenty months, King Euric was struck down by a terrible wasting disease. He died in hideous agony. After that, the Visgoth Empire crumbled, never to rise again.

'In the old tongue the word for thirty is *Triginta*,' concluded Belikov. 'And the word for silver is, *Argenteous*.'

'The *Triginta Argenteous*,' said Jebe, his voice almost throbbing with awe. 'But tell me, my master,' he continued. 'If it comes with such a curse, what use is it to you?'

Belikov laughed. And for the first time in many decades Jebe saw true humor in his expression. 'My good friend,' he answered. 'What is the threat of death to the Undead? No, I can wield the *Triginta* without fear.

'To me it is the key to the kingdom of the world. The path to total control.

'So, Jebe, my true and trusted advisor and companion, we need to bend all effort to tracking it down. Spare no expense, spare no time and accept no excuses. The *Triginta* must be mine.'

Jebe bowed deeply to his king and master, filled with the desire to serve.

And to become the right hand of the future leader of the known world.

CHAPTER 26

Emily was surprised to discover she actually owned a villa in Nice, courtesy of Sylvian's estate.

Muller had been discussing finding a place for the team to stay when Emily had checked her laptop, as the name of the town rang a bell. And, sure enough, there it was. In the area of Old Nice, overlooking the sea.

There was also a contact name and cell number with the address. Emily phoned it and a woman answered. After Emily had informed her who she was, the woman, Sara LaBell, informed her that the villa would be ready for them when they arrived. That included food and servants.

They set off as the sun rose, aiming to get to Nice by late afternoon.

When they pulled up to the gates of the villa they were staggered at its splendor. The house was set in a manicured garden and surrounded by a white rendered wall. They entered through a set of gates that had obviously been opened ready for their arrival, and proceeded up the crushed marble driveway.

The two-story villa was yards from its own private beach with an unobstructed view of both the sea and the town.

The team exited the vehicle to be greeted by a tiny, sophisticated looking, middle-aged woman and two diminutive servants. The servants took their bags while the woman introduced herself.

'*Bonne après-midi*. I am Sara LaBell. I used to be the proxy for *Monsieur* Baptiste in this area. Now I am yours,' she addressed Emily. 'The servants have prepared the villa; cook is preparing an early dinner and I am sure you will want to freshen up. I will show you to your rooms.'

They followed her into the villa.

The entrance hall was a study in wealth and good taste. Cool marble floors, walls and pillars. On the wall, a lost Monet. Waterlilies at dawn. Sweeping stairway up to the second floor.

They ascended the stairs and Sara showed each of them to their rooms.

Emily opened the door to her suite to be greeted by a veritable forest of fresh flowers, a fruit bowl and a selection of snacks laid out on a table. Somehow, even though the servants had been only seconds ahead of them, their clothes were already hanging in the closets.

Emily turned to thank Sara, but she was no longer there.

Troy grinned. 'That girl is not human,' he noted. 'She smells wrong.'

'Neither are the servants,' added Emily. 'No one puts clothes away that fast. Most likely they're some sort of Fae. Brownies, maybe.'

'I thought Brownies were wizened and hairy,' said Troy.

Emily shook her head. 'No, you get all shapes and sizes. Merlin told me about them.' As she talked, she walked across the room and opened the door to the bathroom.

She squealed with excitement. The bathroom was huge. A massive rolltop bath, a walk-in shower. A selection of soaps and potions and unguents that only a girl could appreciate.

Next to the bath, a set of shelves with a pile of fluffy, white towels and bathrobes.

Em turned the faucets on and hot water gushed out like a steaming, indoor Niagara Falls.

Troy helped himself to an apple and opened the doors to the balcony. He stood outside and lit up, knowing he had lost Emily to her ablution's. There was no way he was getting her out of the bath for at least an hour, so he made himself comfortable and settled in for the wait.

***

The dining table was laid with the finest crockery and cutlery.

Tag stared at the vast array of utensils in front of him, a look of consternation on his face. He recognized the knives and the forks and the spoons. But there were other accoutrements he had never seen before. And he had no idea what they might be used for. Some sort of pliers, a tiny little fork with only two prongs, a small mother-of-pearl spoon that looked like it was made for a doll's house.

Sara entered the room and placed a few opened bottles of wine on the table.

'Welcome,' she greeted. 'I was unsure of what you might want for dinner, so I instructed the chef to cook *monsieur* Baptist's favorite dishes. I'm sure you will enjoy them.'

As she left the room, a waiter glided in. He was carrying a silver tray that held a large cone of crushed ice. On the top of the miniature ice mountain was a small glass receptacle.

With practiced hand he scooped a spoonful of the contents onto each person's plate, followed it with a couple of crackers and then left.

Tag frowned. 'What's this black stuff?'

'Caviar,' said Emily.

'What's caviar when it's at home?'

'Fish eggs,' explained Em. 'You use the little mother-of-pearl spoon to put some on a cracker. Then you eat it.'

'Do we have to?'

Muller chuckled. 'Try some. It's not bad.'

Tag scooped a small portion onto a cracker, plopped it into his mouth and chewed. Then he shrugged. 'Fishy.'

'Fishy?' asked Muller. 'That's all you got to say about one of the most expensive delicacies in

117

the world?'

'Expensive?' asked Tag.

'Over a thousand dollars a pound.'

Tag shook his head. 'Stupid.'

The next course arrived shortly after. Tag folded his arms across his chest. 'Oh, come on. No way. Is this for real?'

In front of him, in their shells, were half a dozen snails in garlic butter.

'It's snails,' said Emily.

'Hey, girly, I know what it is. I seen them in the garden before. What I mean is, are we meant to eat them?'

'You use the tongs to hold the shell,' said Emily. 'And then the little silver fork to get them out.'

Tag shook his head.

'They're okay,' said Troy.

'Sure,' snapped Tag. 'You a wolf. You eat raw animals and stuff. I ain't gonna trust you on what's good to chow. Tag is gonna give this one a hard pass.'

'Suit yourself,' said Troy. 'If you aren't going to eat them, pass the plate over.'

Tag slid the snails over to the wolfman with a shudder.

The next course arrived. Huge steaming plate-fuls of it.

'This is tripe,' said Troy. 'Sheep's guts.'

Tag grinned. 'I know, wolfy. Us Jamaicans love our tripe 'n beans.' The big man attacked his plate like a starving trencherman, using his spoon to shovel it in. Before the others had gotten half way through their plates, Tag was banging the table to get seconds. Then thirds.

Next came dessert. A mountain of light, fluffy, sweet cream and chocolate eclairs.

And finally, a selection of cheeses.

Tag leaned back in his chair and burped. 'Exsqueeze me,' he chuckled. 'Man, that started off not so well and ended real good. I'm so full I could explode.'

Troy selected a cigar from a humidor one of the waiters brought in, then he passed the selection to Muller and Tag.

He didn't bother offering Emily as he knew she didn't smoke.

'Let's take the rest of the evening off,' said Emily. 'Tomorrow, we get an early start and do a bit of reconnaissance. Scope out our target and go from there.'

CHAPTER 27

The next warehouse was situated in a small, light industrial complex a mile outside the Nice town borders. A few of the buildings were occupied, and there were signs of some people. A couple of cars. A motorbike.

A faded sign outside the complex stated in French and English that the compound was scheduled for demolition, and was to be replaced by something called a mini-industrial-hive. Whatever the hell that was.

But the sign was at least three or four years old, and there was no trace of any work being done.

And if you looked closely at the target warehouse, you could see that it wasn't nearly as run-down as it initially seemed. The dirt on the windows was actually spray-paint. The ragged roof was still obviously water tight, and the roller doors showed signs of recent use, the hinges and gears well oiled. There were also fresh tire tracks heading into the warehouse via the roller doors.

'Very clever,' said Muller. 'If we hadn't been given this address there's no way we would have found the place.'

'There's a lot of people in the back part of the structure,' said Troy. 'I can smell them. They haven't bathed for a while. And, they stink of fear.'

'I'll go in through the back,' said Emily. 'That way, I can protect the prisoners and keep them calm. You guys hit the front and sides. Tag, front door, Muller go left. Troy, right.'

Tag nodded but didn't answer. He was still sulking because Emily had told him he couldn't bring Missus Jones to the party. She had also insisted both Tag and Muller use suppressors on their firearms. This was because, although there were not hundreds of potential observers, there were some. And Emily did not want to get innocents dragged into the operation for any reason. Even if it was as witnesses after the fact.

As a result, Muller swopped out his usual sawn-off shotgun for a Heckler and Koch sub-machine gun. Unlike the last place the team had hit, a full volume firefight in the warehouse would most definitely attract unwanted attention.

For the same reasons, Emily had also decided Troy should stay in his human form. Just in case someone spotted him.

Troy carried a pair of Maxim Nines. Semi-auto pistols with integral suppressors. And although nothing actually silences a pistol to the point Hollywood would have us believe, it did reduce the volume to an acceptable level. Maybe as loud as a bible dropped onto a wooden table.

While they all headed to their assigned points of entry, Emily headed around to the rear of the warehouse, keeping low and out of sight. They hadn't bothered to synchronize watches or have any form of countdown; the plan was simple. Get in and kill the guards. Emily asked they attempt to keep at least one of the enemy alive for questioning. Because she knew this was only the beginning. And she was determined to track down and destroy all aspects of this corrupt and evil trafficking in human lives.

There was no rear entrance, but there were a series of windows, all covered with steel shutters. Emily eased her fingers under the edge of the first shutter and slowly took the strain. The steel began to deform and then, with a sharp pop, the rivets gave way.

She stopped and listened, checking if the noise had alerted anyone. After a full minute, she deemed it okay to continue and, flexing her muscles, she bent the steel shutter upwards until there was enough room to ingress.

Clambering over the sill, she entered a dark room.

A row of bunk beds was bolted to the one wall. Opposite, an empty chemical toilet. The place reeked of sweat and human waste and harsh antiseptic cleaning products.

There were no people, but she could hear voices from the room next door. But even her heightened hearing couldn't make out the words. Whoever it was, they were murmuring. Low, hoarse whispers.

She could smell their fear. A rank combination of cold sweat overlaid with an iron tang.

Walking softly, she crossed the room and listened at the door, checking if anyone was stationed outside.

Nothing, so she twisted the handle and pushed the door open, finding herself in a dimly lit corridor, no natural lighting, only a couple of energy saving globes. There were three more doors similar to the one she had just exited through.

Without moving, her extraordinary senses told her two of the rooms were occupied, the third empty.

Then her ears picked up the dull thud of Tag's suppressed Desert Eagles, followed immediately by a short scream that cut off as a gurgle. Muller's sword at work.

Grasping the first doorhandle, Emily twisted until the lock popped, then she opened the door and walked in.

The first thing that struck her was the stink of the overflowing chemical toilet. The next was how overcrowded the room was, and she wondered why they didn't simply put some of the prisoners into one of the empty rooms.

The room was full of females. No men. Obviously, their captors had segregated the sexes. The girls cowered as far away from the door as possible. Some glanced at Emily, but most stared at the floor, too terrified to look up.

'Hi,' said Emily. 'Please, don't be scared. I'm here to get you out. I'm a friend.'

Still the girls cringed away from her, and she could hear their hearts beating and their breath rasping in their throats.

'I promise,' continued Emily. 'I tell you what,' she continued. 'You all wait here. I'm going to open the next door and then we'll all leave together. Don't worry about the people who took you, my friends are making sure they never do that to anyone ever again.'

Then the Daywalker backed out of the room, stepped over to the next door and opened it in the same fashion. Brute strength overcoming the lock with ease.

The room was identical. But in this case, there were perhaps half the number of occupants. It seemed that the flesh-traders either preferred females or simply found them easier to kidnap.

The men were not quite as cowed as the girls. The mere fact that they were not as packed together and their chemical toilet had yet to overflow meant they had a little more fire left in them. But not enough to challenge anyone.

'Hey, guys,' greeted Emily. 'Listen up, I'm here with friends. We've come to take you home. Follow me, we need to pick up the girls and get out of here.'

Two of the men had a brief chat and Emily

picked up that at least one of them didn't speak English. So, she quickly repeated her message in French, Italian and German.

There was a collective sigh of relief from all present and they followed her back to the girls' room. Then she took all of them to the window where she had gained entry and, with another display of brute force that caused a collective intake of breath from the prisoners, she tore off the steel shutter and punched out the window to allow an easy exit.

'Right,' she instructed. 'Wait here, all of you. If you go traipsing off and we can't find you when we're done, you'll miss the bus. So, stay. Sit down, below the window line and keep quiet. I'm going back in. Trust me, I won't be long and then we'll get you out of here.'

And with that, Emily jumped back in, looking for the flesh traders.

Time for some retribution.

CHAPTER 28

'I asked you not to kill this one,' snapped Muller.

Tag scowled. 'Didn't mean to.'

'Tag, you hit him so hard his head literally exploded.'

'Hey, he stabbed me,' argued the big man.

'So what? You're always getting stabbed. It's no reason to burst someone's head.'

Tag folded his arms in front of his chest and stuck his bottom lip out like a sulky toddler. 'Hell, you can't bring Missus Jones, don't punch people inna head, do this, do that. I've had enough, you take point then.'

Muller rolled his eyes. 'Fine, I'll take point.'

Tag shook his head and stepped in front of the Knight. 'No. Tag takes point, because he be fine if he gets stabbed. Or shot. Sorry, I know the girly asked us to keep a few alive. I'll make more of an effort.'

The big man had entered through the front door via his usual method. *Id Est*, smashing it into kindling as he simply charged through it. Then he proceeded to exterminate everyone he came across. By the time he met up with Muller they had taken out seven people between them.

In the background they could hear Troy's nine mil's double tapping as he took down a few more.

Then the two of them proceeded towards the rear of the warehouse, wending their way through office partitions, storage areas and bathrooms, killing as they went.

Now they were hoping they hadn't run out of live targets, because Emily would be pissed if they killed everyone and there was no one left to question.

Especially since she had basically given them a direct order. And they both knew from experience – when Emily Hawk, Daywalker, pack member, werewolf, Shadowhunter and leader of the gargoyles, gave you an order, well, you darn well better follow it.

Someone fired at them from behind one of the desks in an open partition. The slug creased Tag's arm. The big man ran towards the source of the shot. As he did, Muller shouted out.

'Don't kill him.'

Another shot rang out, but went high. And then Tag was on him. Throwing the desk out of the way, the big man grabbed the gunman's arm and twisted, forcing him to drop his pistol. At the same time, he gave him a compound, green twig fracture that splintered his arm so badly it flopped down like it had been deboned.

Muller ran up and used zip-ties to strap the man's arms and legs together, handling him roughly, caring not a jot for his injury. Then he ripped the front of the man's shirt off and rammed it into his mouth as a gag.

'Good job,' the Knight said to Tag. 'Let's see if we can find another.'

They left the hapless guard lying on the floor and moved on.

Before they came across anyone else, they ran into Troy. He was carrying an unconscious guard over his left shoulder while holding one of his pistols in his right hand.

'Hey,' said Tag. 'You got one. We got one as well.' He looked at Troy's captive and snorted. 'Ours is bigger than yours.'

'Not a competition,' said Troy.

'Whatever. Just saying.'

Tag went back to pick up his captor and when he returned Emily was with them.

She patted Tag on the back. 'Well done,' she praised him. 'You managed to keep one alive.'

Tag beamed. 'Yeah, and he shot me. But I still didn't punch his head off.'

'Right, guys,' said Emily. 'I freed the prisoners, snuck them out the back through a window. They're waiting there for us. Ran into another two guards on the way here. Sadly, after seeing the way they treated those prisoners, I wasn't as controlled as Tag. So, they're both dead. And sort of in pieces.

'Muller, can I leave you and Tag to question these two while Troy and I take care of the kidnappees?'

The Knight nodded his affirmation. 'I'll text the okay to the local priest. I spoke to him last night and he's got transport, a doctor and a few nuns ready to help. How many?'

'About thirty. Twenty girls, ten guys. Most of the girls are in really bad condition. Staved, dehydrated and abused. The guys are a little better off.'

'I'll tell him,' said Muller. 'You go. The big man and I will wring these two dry.'

'I'll catch up with you,' said Troy. 'I want to go through whatever papers, laptops, computers I can find. That okay?'

Emily nodded. 'Let's get to it, gentlemen. Meet out front when you're finished.'

CHAPTER 29

'Smirnov wasn't here,' said Tag. 'Apparently, he spends most of his time in Paris. Living the high life.'

Emily watched the victims file onto a bus the local church had hired, courtesy of her apparently unlimited funds. Some of the girls needed help walking. One was on a stretcher, a drip attached to her arm

Emily had spoken to a few of the group and she was doing all she could to contain her righteous anger. Many of the girls and some of the boys had been sexually molested. A few had been tortured. For no reason other than a couple of the guard's sick and perverted concepts of pleasure.

After she heard the stories, she returned to the two guards still alive and, ensuring Muller had gotten all he could from them, she summoned Deathwalker and dismembered them.

No one attempted to stop her.

'As soon as these people are comfortable, we find out more about this Smirnov character,' said Emily. 'Like where he lives.'

Muller nodded. 'I already have all of my contacts working on it. Don't worry, we'll find him.'

'And then we kill him,' said Emily. 'Slowly.'

Tag frowned and walked over to the young girl. 'Hey, baby-girl,' he said. 'You know what Tag's main goal in life is? It's to protect you. Your life before mine, always. You know that?'

Emily nodded.

'It's not just physical though. You be careful now, beware the darkness. You know how you can get. Remember why we do what we do. It's not revenge, it's vengeance.'

Emily turned to face the big man and he took an involuntary step back; such was the strength of her anger. The power of her coercion was a physical thing. A mental bludgeon that she sometimes wielded without knowing. And sometimes, without caring. Because, with Emily Hawk, the dark was always close. A part of her she fought against constantly.

Then she saw the look on her friends face and she wilted. 'Sorry, Tag,' she said. 'You have saved my life so many times now I can't count. I don't mean to lash out like that, it's just that I'm so angry. How can people act like that? Torture, rape. Selling people as food?'

'They didn't know,' interjected Muller. 'Obviously they knew about the rape and stuff, I mean they didn't know about the vampires. They thought they were involved in simple people trafficking. Sex trade. Slavery.'

'They are still evil,' insisted Emily.

'I agree,' concurred the Knight. 'And they have been justly punished. Now, we find the head of the snake and cut it off.'

Emily smiled.

CHAPTER 30

Jebe put together a small strike force. Five members. One Chernobyl elite. One assistant *Nosferatu* of at least Adept level. Plus, three qualified familiars.

His game plan was to make many of these teams send them out across Europe, tasking them with tracking down the *Triginta Argenteous.*

But he couldn't just send them in cold. They needed some sort of starting point.

Three Ancients, all over a thousand years old, were present to give advice and share their knowledge. The eldest, Saladin Zaid had been turned one thousand eight hundred years ago, as a twenty-year-old man living in Palestine.

The other two ancients had lived in Germania some thousand years ago when they were turned.

The three of them had caucused together and between them were listing any information they could that might pertain to either the Great Betrayer, King Euric or the *Triginta.*

To be honest, Jebe was a little disappointed at

the lack of depth of information the three Ancients managed to dredge up. Generally, it was hearsay based on rumors based on even more hearsay. But one had to start somewhere.

Together with the Ancients, Jebe had garnered a further six familiars to assist. None of these were historians. Instead, they were information specialists. Four were international private detectives and two were identical twins, Monique and Mandrake DaCosta, cyber-info experts.

Unfortunately, the relic they were attempting to find was steeped in misinformation and rumor, and hidden by what seemed to be an almost total lack of knowledge.

The cyber-twins were trawling the exhibits and warehoused stocks of every major museum in Europe. This would have been an unsurmountable task but for the fact they had developed an automated program to do the actual trawling. Their time was spent hacking into the respective museums data bases and downloading the software.

They had developed a second program to search chat rooms and emails and social media sites to recognize any mention of a list of keywords that might relate to the relic.

The major problem with this was not lack of information – rather it was a surfeit of the stuff. A veritable info-overload. Already, the twins had requested a few assistants. Jebe had sent for an army of them. After all, there was no shortage of familiars. People frantic to share in the *Nosferatu* version of immortality. Desperate to become more than they were.

Of course, most of them were mere wannabees. Goth teenagers, social misfits and pariahs. On the whole, these would all end up as food, after they had performed whatever useful tasks assigned them.

But some were worthy of more careful contemplation. Scholars, warriors, leaders. These would be promoted within the organization and after a while, tried, tested and weighed as to the possibility of being turned.

Those were the sort of people Jebe was using for his quest.

At the moment, the twins had given Jebe three possible targets. Two museums and one private collection. All were in Germany. He immediately dispatched three of the detectives to the source in order to get more intel.

He spent the next twenty minutes or so ensuring that the twins had all they needed to keep researching and, as he was about to leave, one of his *Nosferatu* Adept lieutenants ran in.

'Sir, I have an urgent message from Pytor Smirnov.'

Jebe frowned. Smirnov was a man he did not like. A mere grocer in the scheme of things. Nevertheless, he was important to the house in that he supplied them and many of their allies and future allies with food. Human livestock. As such, he qualified as an ally himself.

'Talk to me,' commanded Jebe.

'His warehouse in Nice has been hit,' informed the Adept. 'Wiped out. All of the stock has been taken. He is worried that his men may have talked, and whoever did this will come for him. He is already well protected by his own men; however, he is afraid,' the vampire concluded, unable to hide the scorn in his voice.

Jebe raised an eyebrow. 'Well, we cannot have our main supplier exterminated,' he said. 'I shall dispatch a task force to Paris immediately via one of the house jets. Inform him they will arrive tomorrow morning. Tell him to show them the utmost respect and to keep out of their way. Warn him that the team will be led by one of the inner circle. One of the Chernobyl superiors. He will come with another *Nosferatu* and ten familiars. Go.'

The lieutenant bowed deeply and sped to do his duty.

Jebe left the room. He decided he would send Leonid Lebedev. A monster of a vampire who had been savagely deformed by the radiation during the Chernobyl incident. But his strength, speed and dedication to the cause were unprecedented. Also, it would expose Pytor Smirnov to the reality of whom he was dealing with. If the coward was afraid now, he had no idea what real fear was.

But when he met Leonid, that would change.

CHAPTER 31

Emily owned a large apartment in Paris.

In fact, she also owned an apartment in the Fae city of Pareen that was situated underneath Paris. Both were courtesy of Sylvian's legacy.

But instead of staying at either, she booked the team of hunters into an hotel Because, even though it had been a year since the French Blood-born's death, her emotions were still too raw to stay in his old house. A hotel was fine for their needs and far less personal.

And because funds were no problem, she had pushed the boat out.

The Prince De Galles Hotel. Avenue George V, Paris.

She had procured a suite of rooms on the top floor at the outrageous cost of over ten thousand dollars a night. She knew it was an unnecessary expense, but she had the cash, and sometimes you've just got to say – what the hell. It's only money.

Three rooms, all linked by interleading doors. A central dining area, a bar, a small indoor pool and a private, plant filled conservatory.

Troy took one look at the huge double bed in their room, smirked and wiggled his eyebrows at Emily. In turn, she threw a pillow at him.

Muller simply chucked his kit into the room, after taking it from the bellhop, and went to the fully stocked bar for a beer.

Tag was like a kid in a candy store.

'Hey, cool,' he yelled from his room. 'Check it out. Tiny bottles of shampoo. And bath bubbles.' He laughed out loud. 'Teeny soaps. Man, I feel like a giant.' He ran through to Em's suite, holding a bathrobe and a pair of slippers. 'Can we use these?' he asked. 'I mean, is it free?'

Troy chuckled. 'Sure. But I doubt it will fit you. That's the problem with this one-size-fits-all. For you and I, it normally means, one-size-doesn't-fit-all.'

Tag tried pulling the bathrobe on over his shirt, but Troy was correct, it was far too small.

'Darn.'

Emily laughed. 'If you want a robe that fits, I'll buy you one later.'

Tag grinned. 'Cool. I'm hungry. When are we eating?'

'Soon,' answered Emily. 'Apparently they have an amazing sushi restaurant in the hotel.'

Tag frowned. 'Isn't that raw fish?'

Em nodded.

'No way,' said Tag. 'You've already tried to make me eat snails and fish eggs. Now raw fish? No. Let's find a place that serves steak. Huge, bleeding portions. And fries.'

Troy nodded his agreement. 'I'm with the big man. Steak. Rare. Humongous.'

Emily rolled her eyes. 'Fine,' she said. 'Steak. Then we find the target and do a recce.'

Tag gave a thumb up. 'Excellent.'

CHAPTER 32

Leonid Lebedev and his team arrived that morning. Two blacked out SUV's picked them up at a private airport and transported them and their equipment to Smirnov's palatial dwelling on the outskirts of Paris.

Smirnov's residence wasn't geared for the children of the night. There were drapes, but they weren't rubber backed, and many of them didn't even cover the windows enough to prevent the sunlight shining in.

As such, Lebedev had tasked his ten familiars, all of whom were experienced mercenaries, with daylight guard duties.

Lebedev and Karl, his Adept lieutenant, would take care of the night when it was possible for them to roam freely.

When the Smirnov was introduced to the Chernobyl vamp, he quailed visibly. He had been warned to expect someone a little ... different. But when actually confronted by the seven-foot tall, massively muscled, misshapen and deformed creature that was Leonid Lebedev, he lost control of his emotions and literally cowered in fear.

And it didn't help that Lebedev did not make the slightest effort to control his massive powers of glamor. Radiating fear-inducement and contempt like a lighthouse giving off light. To be honest, terrifying the meat to the point of almost senseless terror was one of the only forms of enjoyment left to him.

Gone were the sumptuous balls and parties of old. The hunt and seduction and eventual feasting on beautiful maidens. Not the way he and his Chernobyl brethren now looked.

They had swopped suave sophistication and eternal good looks for terrifying physical deformation and unbelievable levels of power.

And now, as the sun began to crawl behind the horizon, it was his turn to protect the cowardly meat supplier. Personally, he would rather tear him limb from limb and spit on his remains. But the Blood King had ordered his protection, and the *Krov Tsar's* word was the ultimate law.

Nevertheless, Lebedev considered the entire mission to be a waste of time. Smirnov was already extremely well protected. He had over thirty well-armed and experienced bodyguards. All ex-special forces, mainly Russian *Spetsnaz* with a sprinkling of Israeli *Sayeret* and even a couple of South African Recces. No force of less than company strength would be capable of even getting close to him.

Lebedev lit a cigarette. He could no longer

really taste them, but he had been smoking for over two hundred years, and the familiar movements and rigmarole brought him a minuscule of comfort. He could have smoked the finest, hand rolled Turkish cigarettes if he were so inclined. But instead, Lebedev smoked Russian Belomorkanals. The strongest cigarette ever made. And the cheapest. Constructed from cardboard and fifth grade tobacco, they smelled like a burning pile of manure.

And Lebedev was vaguely amused at the distaste he registered on others faces when he lit the execrable tubes of tabaco and filled the room with the foul-smelling smoke.

Small pleasures.

The vampire took a final drag, dropped the butt on the carpet and ground it in with his heel. He was about to light another when, despite the onerous reek of the cheap tabaco, he smelled it. A scent so ingrained he could never mistake it. Although, to be fair, this one was a little different. Less animal. More human.

Werewolf.

He reacted instantly, calling out to Karl as he sprinted towards the source of the new scent. As he ran, he heard a sound that was so incongruous he almost faltered. It was the sound of a General Electric M134 Minigun spewing out lead at a rate of 6000 rounds a minute.

Part of him thought he must be mistaken. The M134 was a weapon designed to be mounted on a helicopter or armored vehicle. And there had been no sound of any automobile approaching.

The sound of returning small arms fire crackled through the air, and then the Minigun spoke again.

And in the background, Lebedev swore he heard someone shout – *Say hello to Missus Jones.*

Obviously, he must have heard incorrectly.

Turning the corner, he skidded slightly on the marble floor as he entered the entrance hall to the mansion. The place looked like a charnel house. Several bodies were scattered about the hall, blood coated the walls and even the ceiling, and the insanely rapid fire from the Minigun had chewed up walls, chandeliers and furniture.

He heard screaming and growling from down the corridor and at the same time, Karl joined him, blurring across the room to stand next to him.

'I can smell werewolf,' said his lieutenant.

Lebedev nodded his agreement, the movement causing the lumps and tumors on his face to wobble in concert.

Karl who was similarly affected, didn't notice.

Together, they followed the noise.

The battle seemed to be coming from the huge ballroom. The double doors were open and the sounds of small arms fire and cries of both fear and anger reverberated through the building.

Both vampires blurred into the room, crossing behind the local guards and taking cover behind

143

one of the upturned tables. A quick glance belied Lebedev's previous statement that it would take a full company to breach their defenses. It now seemed that what it would actually take was a wolfman, a young blonde supermodel and two humans to do so.

'What is that?' asked Karl.

'Wolfman,' answered Lebedev. 'An Omega werewolf. Very rare. Very dangerous.'

Karl shook his head. 'No,' he said. 'That,' he pointed at Emily.

Lebedev was about to snap at the younger vampire when he actually looked. Karl was correct. What the hell was that? At first glance she appeared to be a normal human female. But if you applied the smallest amount of attention you could immediately sense an aura of unbelievable power. And danger. Almost as if ... no. It wasn't possible.

'She's a vampire,' said Lebedev. 'And an ancient. And something else.'

'I thought she was a werewolf,' answered Karl.

'No, wait. Yes. Could it be *Her?*'

'Do you mean...'

'The Daywalker,' stated Lebedev.

As Lebedev made his statement, the final guard fell to a burst of fire from the Minigun.

A strange ringing silence filled the air.

And the two vampires stood up. The Minigun did not scare them. They knew they were simply too fast to be shot. The only way to take down one of the brethren of Chernobyl was to go old school.

Mano-a-mano.

And when it came to physical combat. The two deformed and overpowered monsters were at the very acme of the class.

'Prepare to die,' declaimed Lebedev.

'Ooh, ugly,' said Tag with a shudder.

CHAPTER 33

Emily saw the two monsters stand up from behind the overturned table and flinched at the sight of them.

They were beyond doubt the most deformed, warped and misshapen creatures she had ever seen. It seemed as though they might once have been human. Or at least humanoid. But now they looked like some sort of troll, sculpted by careless hand and then damaged by vandals.

Humped backs, massive shoulders and arms, faces full of tumorous growths, fingers with too many joints and eyes that blazed bright red.

And huge. The one was at least seven feet tall and must have weighed five hundred pounds.

Both of them radiated an aura of power and great danger. So much so the very air about them shimmered with it.

'They stink of Vampire,' growled Troy. 'But they look like no *Nosferatu* I have seen before.'

Tag opened up with Missus Jones, the Minigun chewing up the table and the wall behind it as it spewed out a hundred rounds in a fraction of a second. But it was to no avail. The two creatures moved so fast it was as if they had teleported. One moment they were behind the table, the next, they had separated to opposite sides of the room.

Emily tensed, ready for battle. Never before had she seen such speed. They were faster than Troy. Maybe even faster than her. Summoning Deathwalker she moved forward.

As did Tag and Muller.

Troy held back slightly, positioning himself on the side, ready to flank them.

None of the hunters had to bother about the human guards. All of the ones on the ground floor had already been dispatched and, although they knew there were more in the mansion, they were as naught compared to the pair of monsters in front of them right now.

Tag dropped Missus Jones and drew his two Desert Eagles, forsaking firepower for maneuverability.

Muller held his sword in his right hand and his shotgun in his left. The two of them advanced on the slightly smaller vamp, leaving the larger one for Em and Troy.

Emily's usual supreme confidence was tempered slightly by the monster's expression. Even through the tumors and hanging wattles of flesh, she could see that he wasn't in the slightest bit nervous, even though he was facing an Omega wolfman and Em, who was also someone of obvious power. In fact, the creature looked keen.

Like he was finally facing an enemy worthy of his attention.

She heard Tag's Eagles thunder and Muller's shotgun boom in concert. Then she heard a meaty thud and, out of the corner of her eye, she saw both Tag and Muller sail across the room and smash into the opposite wall.

A quick glance showed her Muller was out for the count and Tag, who was badly injured, would take a few seconds to recover. But what surprised her the most was that the vamp who had struck the two had moved so fast she didn't sense him attacking.

With a frown she gestured towards the vamp who had just dispatched her friends. 'Troy, take him. I'll get this one.'

She saw Troy attack and at the same time she moved forward, Deathwalker held in both hands, ready to rock and roll.

Her opponent leered at her. 'Daywalker, I presume.'

Emily didn't answer. She was there to fight, not exchange pleasantries. Piling on the speed, she ran forward and flicked the axe at the monster's head, spinning as she did so to ensure her back wasn't exposed.

The creature's response took her by total surprise. She expected him to dodge. Perhaps lean away from the blow or duck underneath. As such, she followed her swing and spin with a low-level kick, hoping to sweep his legs.

Instead, he leaped into the air, raking his talons along Emily's face as he did. Blood sprayed across the room and Emily dropped and rolled to avoid any follow up strike. But the monster moved with her, anticipating her move and stamping down on her as she rolled.

Emily felt her ribs break as the monster's foot landed, but remembering Bastian's instructions, she kept moving. To be still was to die. Throwing herself forward, she performed a half twist and hit the wall with both feet, flexing and springing back, the axe in front of her as she did.

Again, the deformed vampire shifted to one side, but Emily's athleticism had taken him by surprise and the point of one of the butterfly shaped blades bit deep into his right shoulder.

Meanwhile, Troy had his plate full with the second vampire. This fight was different. Eschewing fast moves and athletic spins, the Wolfman and the vampire stood toe-to-toe and traded blows, their surfeit of testosterone overwhelming any sense of tactics. This was merely two males battling for dominance. And usually, Troy would be more than happy to take part in such a basic, strength heavy contest. After all, he was Omega.

But for the first time in his life, he was shocked at his opponent's strength. And speed.

If he was entirely honest with himself, he would have to admit the vampire shaded him in both departments. But he was Omega, and

149

the Pack leader would never admit he was out-gunned. Not to his friends, not to his pack, not to his team mates.

And never to himself.

Redoubling his efforts, the wolfman fought back with all he had.

Emily circled her creature, feinting every now and then with Deathwalker, trying to draw the vampire into a false move. However, he was a wily opponent, ancient beyond Emily's imagination, and his experience covered thousands of battles.

But Emily was a combination of two of the *Nosferatu's* most dedicated mortal enemies. Werewolf and Shadowhunter. She was also – Daywalker. So, what she lacked in experience she made up for in sheer skill and talent.

And where Lebedev had fought both man, and vampire and werewolf before, he had never fought anyone who was a combination of the deadliest parts of all three.

Lebedev glanced down at the wound in his shoulder. It wasn't that deep and should have healed up almost instantly. But for some reason it was still bleeding.

Emily chuckled. 'Meet Deathwalker,' she said. 'You will find it's not so easy to heal from his wounds, you evil bloodsucker.' Then she swung the axe in a complicated series of cuts and slashes, displaying an awesome control of the weapon.

But Lebedev was less than impressed. 'Ah, the arrogance of youth,' he noted. 'Child, I have faced some of the best axe men in the world. I have fought on the walls of Constantinople and in the vastness of the Steppes. Your paltry skills are as naught to me.'

And to prove his point, he shifted behind Emily and once again his talons tore deeply into her.

She flicked out with her axe, but he had already moved out of her reach.

Part of her attention picked up on Troy. For some reason he was standing head-to-head with the other twisted vampire and trading blows like some sort of kindergarten-based macho-man contest.

Tag had recovered and was reloading his pistols.

Muller lay still, but breathing, lights out.

Lebedev continued moving, walking in a slow circle around Emily. In turn, she spun her axe in a figure eight, waiting for him to strike.

She heard Tag's Eagles boom and then Troy growled. 'Hey, stop that. This one's mine.'

A flicker of a grin crossed Emily's face. Boys!

As the vampire moved around her, Emily figured she had the edge on him when it came to maneuverability. On the other hand, he was as fast, if not faster, and definitely stronger. Which was extremely disconcerting. She had fought Ancients and Masters before, and none of them had come close to her in any of the aforementioned traits.

With that in mind, Emily flexed her legs and sprang upwards, somersaulting over the monster and slashing down with her axe as she did. The blades caught him on the side of his head, cutting deeply. But his skull was covered so thickly in lumps and growths the axe didn't actually penetrate to the skull. As Emily landed, she could see the wound was already closing, despite Deathwalker's power.

And for the first time in a while, she felt a tiny shimmer of doubt. She knew she could beat this monster, yet not as easily as she had become accustomed.

Lebedev placed his hands on his hips and laughed out loud. He seemed genuinely amused, but in all fairness, it was difficult to tell, such was the horror of his visage.

'I have heard stories of you,' he announced. 'The Daywalker. The Shadowhunter. The Pack member who killed one of our most powerful brethren. How disappointing the reality is. How banal and predictable you are. A monkey doing acrobatics, when I expected a warrior. You disgust me, little girl.'

Emily felt her anger rise. How dare this bloodsucking leech say she was disgusting? A monster that literally murdered humans to live. The epitome of selfish evil.

With a gesture she banished Deathwalker. Her

anger was such that she needed to use her hands. Her talons and teeth. She wanted to get down and dirty with this monster. And not in a good way.

With a conscious effort, Emily dropped her barriers and allowed her dark side to gain ascendency.

Her jaw elongated slightly, and her vampire-canines grew. Talons extended from her fingers and her muscles swelled. Her eyes shone redly and a thin layer of fur covered her arms.

She was now a perfect blend of the most powerful aspects of her various powers. And it was most definitely a case of the sum of the parts was more than the whole. A practical example of perfect synergy.

Bloodlust rushed to her head, almost overwhelming her with the desire ... no, the *need* to kill. It was a feeling Emily had been desperately trying to avoid, because she knew, that way lay madness.

And then it was there, and she was filled with the divine madness of battle.

Lebedev flinched when he saw the change come over her, her aura changing from deadly warrior to insane berserker.

With a screech of anger, Emily threw herself at the monster.

Lebedev moved, putting all he had into his speed. But it was like Emily was just that microsecond ahead of him. Like she could see into the future. Wherever he turned, she was there, with tooth and claw and blood.

Lebedev's composure cracked as the Daywalker began to tear him apart. Bones splintered, huge slabs of flesh were sliced from his body, fingers were ripped from his hands and his skull shattered as Emily piledrove her fists into the back of his head.

After mere seconds of hyper-fast combat, Lebedev fell to his knees, his awesome powers of recovery insufficient to keep up with the savage beating he was taking.

Emily stood over him, talons outstretched towards his face.

And he looked up at her. And nodded. He had been fairly beaten.

'Well done, Daywalker' he said, genuinely impressed. 'Unfortunately,' he continued. 'I am but one of many. And I am not even the most powerful amongst us. When the *Krov Tsar* descends upon you with all of his house, you will stand no chance.'

Emily sneered at the vanquished monster and with a final flourish, she called forth Deathwalker and swung the blades down.

Lebedev's head leaped off his shoulders and rolled across the room.

CHAPTER 34

Troy flicked out a quick combination, tagging the vampire with a flurry of blows to his head.

In return, the vampire launched a massive roundhouse kick. The wolfman hunkered down and took the hit. The power of the kick rocked him back on his feet and he grunted in pain.

Then the two of them stepped apart as if by prior agreement, both allowing themselves time to heal.

Troy held a warning hand up to Tag who was itching to unleash his Desert Eagles on the monster. The wolfman was determined to take the creature by himself.

He was about launch himself back into the fight when he saw, out of the corner of his eye, the Knight of the Holy See rise to his feet and shake his head.

Muller took one look at the vampire facing Troy and with surprising speed, hauled a glass flask from his webbing and threw it at the creature.

'The power of Christ compels me,' he shouted.

The flask of Holy Water shattered against the

vampire's tumor encrusted head and immediately started to burn him, the power of light scorching deep into the evil entities lumpen flesh. Karl shrieked, a long-drawn-out sound like a steam whistle, only deeper. Then he fell to his knees, clawing at his face, shredding his own flesh in an attempt to stop the burning.

'Oh come on,' yelled Troy. 'I told you guys; that one was mine.'

Muller, who had just regained consciousness, looked baffled.

With a sigh of discontent, Troy grabbed the screaming vampire by his head and twisted, snapping his neck and then, with one more mighty heave, tearing his head off and dropping it to the floor to partner Lebedev's detached cranium.

Tag walked up to the pair of heads and emptied his Eagles into them, reducing them to little more than slightly spherical lumps of mashed flesh and bone.

'What was that for?' asked Troy.

The big man shrugged. 'These monsters were seriously gnarly,' he answered. 'Just wanted to make sure they didn't reconstitute or nothing.'

'Fair enough,' conceded the wolfman.

Emily drew a deep breath as Troy approached her.

'You okay?' he asked.

She nodded. 'Yep. Just need to center myself. Then we find Smirnov and get rid of the rest of his guards.'

'Cool,' responded the wolfman. 'Tell us when you're good to go.'

Tag took out a roll of bandage and proceeded to wrap the wound on Muller's head, staunching the slow but steady flow of blood.

'Those things were bad,' said Muller.

'No crap?' quipped Tag. 'They dodged Missus Jones and then put the slap down on you and me like we was little chillun. Been a while since I been manhandled like that. And Troy's less than happy 'cause you Holy-watered his one.'

'Not my fault,' said Muller. 'I came to, saw the wolfman battling it out and thought I'd give him a hand. Didn't know he'd called shotgun.'

Tag chuckled. 'Don't sweat it. That feel better?'

Muller touched the bandage and nodded. 'Got a headache, but that will pass.'

'I'm ready,' interjected Emily. 'Let's find this murdering slave trader and make him wished he was never born.'

The team followed Emily as she exited the ballroom. Troy stuck close behind her, his nose checking ahead of them, ensuring no one tried to ambush the team.

There was no one left alive downstairs and it was obvious the rest of the personal protection squad had closed in around their boss and were most likely ensconced in a defendable area or room.

They proceeded up the stairs and started a room-to-room search.

Calls of, 'clear', sounded out as they went through the rooms.

No one was present.

They worked their way up to the top floor, climbing the stairway which opened out into a large lobby or landing. The area was vast, and most of it was covered in small groups of potted plants. Everything from shrubs to flowers to small trees. Nestled in amongst the jungle of plants were occasional chairs, coffee tables and fish tanks filled with tropical fish. At the far right stood a large aviary. Parrots, Cockatoos, Budgies and various other varieties of brightly feathered birds.

Tag nodded in approval. 'Nice,' he said. 'It's like being outside when you're inside. I like it.'

Muller snorted. 'I've always been of the belief that houses were invented to keep the outside where it belongs. Not for me, sharing my home with random fauna and flora.'

'Boys,' said Emily. 'Concentrate. Troy, what's your nose tell you? Where are they?'

The wolfman tested the air. 'There,' he growled. 'Behind the big bird cage thing.'

'Aviary,' corrected Muller.

'Whatever.'

They walked over to the aviary, and sure enough, there was a concealed door behind it. The cage itself was shaped to provide easy access.

Emily ran her hand over it. 'Cold,' she observed. 'Feels like its steel. Thick. Can't see how it locks. Must be electronic. Maybe Tag could break it down, probably not.'

The big man patted Missus Jones. 'Got five hundred rounds here that beg to differ,' he said.

Muller stepped forward and examined the door carefully. Then he took out a dagger and scored the wall on the right-hand side, etching a line in the plaster. 'Shoot there,' he told Tag. 'It will do no good firing at the door itself; we need to destroy the hinges and their mountings.'

Tag nodded. 'Block you ears,' he warned, and he depressed the trigger. The roar of the Minigun filled the room sending the birds into a frantic cacophony of terrified noise. Five hundred rounds of 7.72mm FMJ tore into the wall, chewing up the plaster and splitting the brickwork behind it.

As the barrels of the gatling gun spun to a halt, Emily tapped Troy on the shoulder. 'Hit it,' she commanded.

Four hundred pounds of wolfman ran shoulder first into the steel door, tearing it from its weakened housing and punching it into the room.

Two assault rifles opened up as the door hit the floor. Troy took three rounds to the chest while the rest of the slugs ricocheted off the walls behind him. He fell to the floor as his flesh started to heal.

Missus Jones was out of ammo, so Tag drew his Eagles and fired at the pair of assailants. Muller joined in, his shotgun booming out its defiance.

The two shooters were thrown across the room by the concentrated firepower. Emily followed up with Deathwalker, decapitating both of them in swift succession.

And then there was one.

A short, unprepossessing man, shaped like a pear with twig-like arms, thick eyeglasses, an obvious toupee and an expensive suit. Tears ran down his cheeks.

Emily walked up to him. 'Smirnov?'

He nodded.

'Right,' she said. 'This is how things are going to happen. You will tell me everything you can about your operation. People, places, bank details – everything. Every time you hesitate or I suspect you are withholding information,' she held up Deathwalker. 'I remove a finger. Understand?'

The Russian nodded.

An hour later Emily looked at Muller. 'Anything else you can think of?'

The Knight shook his head.

'Troy, Tag?'

They both emulated Muller's response.

Emily nodded and raised the axe high.

'Mercy?' whimpered Smirnov.

'Sorry,' replied Emily. 'We're fresh out.'

And the blades dropped.

CHAPTER 35

Gunter Meyer called himself a private detective. He was based in Munich, Germany and worked out of a small office situated in one of the less fashionable areas of the city. He had no staff but didn't work alone, as he often used outside contractors.

Because, although Gunter referred to himself as a private detective, a more accurate description might have been, industrial spy. Or sometimes even, a procurer of wanted items presently owned by someone else.

Basically, a thief and an infiltrator.

But Gunter was not an assassin. For that, and for various other jobs that required a more physical approach, he used outside help.

This was one of those other jobs.

Gunter had been tasked by his primary, a man he had never met but knew as, Jebe Zurgadai, to find out whether a certain someone had a certain antiquity in their possession.

The person in point was a man known to all as, *Die Kettensage.* Or in English, the Chainsaw.

And the Chainsaw was not the sort of man you

crossed. Or at least, not the sort of man you got caught crossing.

The antiquity was described as a necklace or torc made from a series of silver Roman Denarias circa 33AD. It was rumored that the Chainsaw had the said necklace in his possession.

Gunter was not surprised. The Chainsaw was well, known for his huge collection of art and antiquities. The man was obsessed with them. Gunter knew for a fact that the gangster owned at least one lost Chagall and two Picassos. All gained illegally and displayed openly in his mansion.

The necklace of Roman coins, however, was allegedly kept in a strongroom that doubled as a display area for the Chainsaw's most treasured items. Gunter had checked with various reliable sources and they had confirmed the Chainsaw did indeed own some sort of object crafted from Roman Denaria. Gunter was sure it could be little else than what Jebe was seeking.

Bearing this in mind, he hired a team he had used before. A crack selection of safe busters, cat burglars and strongarm men. Six all in all. Then he paid them an obscene amount of money, half up front, to steal the coin necklace. Cost was no object as Jebe had promised almost untold wealth to the person who provided him with the object.

Gunter had no idea why anyone would offer so much for what seemed like a minor treasure, but his was not to reason why, his was simply to obtain the goods and get paid.

And now the only surviving member of the team stood opposite him, bleeding badly from two gunshot wounds. One in his shoulder, the other in his right thigh.

'The only reason I got away was because I was the getaway driver,' said Jonny *'the wheel'* Abel. 'Charlie kept his cell on so I could hear how the operation was playing out. You know, so I could be ready when they exited. But they ran into trouble almost straight away. Some sort of electronic area sensor that wasn't in the blueprints.

'And then the shooting started. Man, it was a real firefight. Everybody shooting at everybody else.

'Finally, they got hold of Charlie. All I could hear was him begging for them not to cut him. Then they started asking him questions ... I couldn't listen any more. The screaming. Man, the screaming. So, I cut the connection and started to drive off. That's when some of the sentries spotted me. Opened up on the car. I was lucky they didn't kill me.'

Gunter sighed. 'Oh well, easy come, easy go,' he said. 'I'm going to take a bit of a financial knock, but that can't be helped.'

Jonny shook his head. 'No, boss,' he said. 'I didn't tell you the worst of it.'

'There's more?'

'For sure. The last thing I heard, just before

I cut the connection was Charlie telling them who hired us. He was screaming out your name. Over and over and over.'

Gunter blanched in fear. 'Oh, crap.' He picked up his cell.

'Boss, I need a doctor,' mumbled Jonny.

'Shut up,' commanded Gunter. 'I need to make this call.'

'Who you phoning?'

'Not your concern,' snapped Gunter. 'But you know the expression, between a rock and a hard place?'

'Yes.'

'That's where I am right now. I've got to explain to someone why I haven't carried out their instructions. And I have a feeling that the consequences might even be worse than the Chainsaw coming for me.'

'Sorry, boss.'

'You and me both, Jonny. You and me both.'

CHAPTER 36

'More Russians,' said Muller.

'So,' responded Tag. 'A lot of the slave trade coming out of Europe is Russian controlled.'

'True,' agreed the Knight. 'But this is getting beyond coincidence. I'm telling you; something is up with the Russians.'

'Gentlemen,' said Emily. 'Not to put too fine a point on it, but what the hell? We've just fought two of the meanest, badest...'

'Butt ugliest,' interjected Tag.

'Yes,' agreed Em. 'Butt ugliest vampires I have ever seen. Or even heard of. Russians, not Russians, who cares? Before I killed the big one, he told me there were many more like him. And that is not good, not good at all. It took everything we had to put those two down, imagine another twenty. Or fifty, or a hundred.'

Muller frowned. 'It matters, Emily. In fact, even more so, because those bad boys we just came up against were Russian. As far as I can deduce, it looks like the Russian *Nosferatu* are looking to expand. Or ally themselves with the French, and most likely the rest of the European brethren. Except, as I said before, that makes no sense. It's like throwing a viper in amongst a pit full of other snakes and asking them to get along. It will never happen.'

'And yet you say it is happening,' Emily pointed out.

Muller grimaced, his face set in an expression of worry. 'Yes,' he admitted. 'And I tell you, it scares me. We need to find out what the hell is going on. And quickly before we're inundated with hordes of those ugly super-vampires.'

'And don't forget, we gotta shut down the rest of Smirnov's operation,' added Tag. 'Who knows how many innocents are being held by his operatives? And time's running short before they all become vampire takeout.'

Emily sighed. 'I'm worried,' she admitted. 'I can feel things are starting to kick off. Something is bubbling under and it could easily spiral out of control. I think we need help.'

'I agree,' concurred Muller. 'But who? The church can only help so much. The new Pope refuses to acknowledge the vampire threat. As it is, I am almost acting unilaterally and without proper support. To push it any further would be counterproductive.'

Emily turned to Troy. 'We need you to summon the packs,' she said.

Troy shook his head.

'Troy, my darling,' continued Emily. 'They are the only ones who can help. Muller is correct, if we don't nip this thing in the bud we could be overwhelmed by those ugly super-vamps.'

'No,' said the Omega wolf. 'Last time we gathered the packs they were almost destroyed. Out of over thirty wolves only seven survived.'

'It is war,' interjected Muller. 'It's what we do. People, wolves, our friends die. It's a sad and terrible truth, but it is what we have chosen.'

Troy shook his head. 'That is true for us. For you, me, Tag, Emily. We chose this path. But as Omega, if I call on the pack, they have to obey. There is no choice. I command, they do. It is as simple as that. I can't have their lives on my conscience, their blood on my soul.'

'What if you gave them, a choice?' asked Emily.

Troy scoffed. 'What choice is there if you know what your Omega actually wants? They will still simply obey. I call, they come, they die. No, I will not do it. Not yet at any rate. Not while there may still be alternatives.'

No one spoke for a while as they let the tension dissipate a little.

Troy lit a cigarette and blew smoke rings towards the ceiling. Muller took out a knife and started to sharpen it with a small whetstone.

Eventually, Tag spoke. 'What about Merlin? Can't we call him?'

'How?' asked Emily. 'He just disappeared after the big battle. Him and the Prof. And it's not like he has a cell. Hell, for all we know he's not even

167

in this world, or even on the same plane of existence.'

'There must be a way,' insisted Tag. 'Just concentrate on him. Maybe he'll hear.'

'He's not a god, Tag,' snapped Emily. 'He's
close, I'll give you that, but he's not omnipotent.'

Tag was about to answer when instead he
frowned.

'It means all-powerful. All seeing. Godlike,' explained Troy. 'The word, omnipotent.'

'I know that,' said Tag. Then he shrugged. 'Sort
of. Not really, thanks. I actually thought it had
something to do with needing Viagra.'

'No, that's impotent,' corrected Troy.

Emily grinned. 'Easy mistake.'

'What about the gargoyles,' continued the big
man, refusing to give up. 'Can't you ask them?
Maybe they've seen Merlin, or maybe they know
something, anything that could help us track
him down.'

A look of guilt flashed across Emily's face. 'It's
been almost a year,' she replied. 'And I haven't
tried to contact any of them. Not Coldstone,
Limerock, none of them.'

'They'll understand,' said Tag. 'After all, what
is a year to those rocky mothers'? Like a day to
us. Give it a go.'

Emily composed herself, emptying her mind,
relaxing. Not quite meditation, but not far off.
Then she pulsed out her call. Seeking the gar-

goyles. A worldwide shout out.

A jumble of sound and vision came back. A busted television, or an old CB radio with a broken transistor. Snippets of sound, half pictures. Static. Feelings of loss.

The wave of meaningless feedback was overwhelming and she felt an immediate migraine start to pound her head. As she stopped concentrating, a voice echoed in her mind. A mere echo of an echo. So faint as to be almost a figment of her imagination.

A voice full of untold torment and pain and fear and sorrow.

And hate.

'Emily Hawk? Is that you?'

Her eyes opened wide and the blood drained from her face. Then the voice was gone.

'What?' asked Troy concernedly. 'Are you okay? What happened?'

'I… nothing. Just noise. Except, at the end. Someone. Or something spoke. I think.'

'Merlin?' asked Tag.

Emily shook her head.

'Who?'

'I think,' answered Emily. 'It was, the Morrigan.'

CHAPTER 37

Gunter had never been so terrified in his life. In fact, the entire concept of terror had been re-wired in his brain.

Not fear.

Fear was such a weak word.

Terror. With a generous helping of horror on the side.

Mind numbing, bowel loosening, mind wiping terror.

Because there are certain things the human mind struggles to process. And hideously deformed undead creatures of the night are most definitely amongst those things.

Up until that evening, Gunter had been unaware of the exact origins and background of his major client. One, Jebe Zurgadai. And if anyone had told him, well, his response would most likely have been – *pull the other one.*

After he phoned Jebe and told him of the disastrous failed attempt at obtaining the artifact, Jebe told him it was unacceptable. Then he informed Gunter he would be dispatching a team of his own to come and sort the problem out.

Gunter had been both pleased and scared. On the one hand, he was getting some extra protection against the Chainsaw, but on the other hand, a team of quite obviously dubious characters were coming to his patch.

The words *frying pan* and *fire* came to mind.

The next evening the team arrived.

And the terror came with it.

The head of the team, or the Adept in charge, as he was called, went by the name of Oblonsky. That was it. No first name.

And he...it...was the most horrendous thing Gunter had ever seen or imagined. His lumpen, deformed and broken visage was such that it would have given Stephen King a heart attack. But his horror inducing appearance wasn't even the worst of it.

No. The worst was his eyes. And the waves of dread that emanated from him like heat off a coal stove. The hatred and horror were so thick it seemed to coat Gunter's very soul. Filling him with dread and revulsion and terror all at the same time.

He was ashamed to admit that he had actually soiled himself when the monster first entered the room and cast his baleful glare at him.

With Oblonsky came five others. One more misshapen one and four humans. And after they arrived, and Gunter had been allowed to clean himself up, they had changed his life.

Now he knew the monsters under the bed

were real. Vampires, werewolves, fae and demons. Gunter's world had come crashing down
around him and his hold on sanity had become
a tenuous thing. In fact, oddly, the only thing
keeping him going was his terror. It was like a
battery to his heart. A constant flood of adren-
aline.

Plus, somewhere in the back of his mind, he
was hoping to wake up and discover the whole
thing had just been a nightmare of epic propor-
tions.

But that was never going to happen.

Now he found himself, at midnight, standing outside *Die Kettensage's* palatial mansion.
The place looked like a cross between modern
brutalist architecture and a maximum-security
prison. All poured concrete, high walls and large
plate glass windows.

Teams of guards patrolled the roof, the garden
and the walls. Access was limited to a single
entrance with a wrought iron gate. To the side,
built into the wall, a guardhouse. The fact that
Charlie's squad had managed to breach the perimeter before they got caught was testament to
their professionalism. Unfortunately, they simply weren't professional enough and had paid
the ultimate price for their failure.

And now Gunter was going in, with Oblonsky
and the second vampire whose name he didn't
know, and two of the human mercenary types.
The humans were dressed in full black combat

gear and carried enough ordnance to start a war. Which was, ostensibly, what they were about to do.

Gunter felt sick with terror. The odds were simply too far against them. How could five men...well, three men and two – things? – hope to get into this fortress and live? Let alone steal the object and egress without being killed.

Impossible.

The vampire squad got out of the vehicle and Oblonsky beckoned to Gunter to follow.

Gunter did so on unsteady legs. He had no idea why he had to be part of the team. After all, he wasn't any sort of wet work specialist. He was basically a researcher, a facilitator. A manager who liked to call himself a detective.

But Oblonsky had insisted. He maintained that as it was Gunter's failure he had to be there when others cleaned up his mess for him.

The detective was convinced this was a suicide mission. However, he was committed and, at the very least, death would bring an end to this new found constant feeling of overwhelming terror.

The team approached the gates, Oblonsky in the lead. Gunter had no idea how the vampire monster thought they were going to get in. it was sure to be a simple case of the gate guards refusing entry. and that would be that.

They stopped at the gate and one of the guards exited the guardhouse and approached. As he saw Oblonsky, he did a classic double take, recoiling from the horror that stood in front of him.

But before the guard could react further, Oblobnsky held his hand up and spoke in a low commanding voice.

'Open the gates. If your compatriot argues, subdue him with all necessary force.'

Oh great, thought Gunter. Not only are these things terrifyingly ugly, they are also insane with delusions of grandeur. Does he really think the guard is simply going to follow his instructions?

But to his amazement, the guard did exactly that. With a look of shock etched on his face, he turned and lurched back to the guardhouse on stiff legs. Like a badly controlled puppet.

Gunter heard a muted argument. Then a single shot rang out and the gate rumbled open.

The vamp squad walked in.

As they did so, the guard lurched back out of the guardhouse and stood before Oblonsky, his pistol still in his right hand.

The vampire monster nodded his acknowledgment of the man's presence.

'Well done,' he told him. 'I have no further use for you. Take your firearm and shoot yourself in the face.'

Gunter watched as the guard struggled to resist whatever it was the vampire monster was doing to him. A sweat broke out and tears rolled down his cheeks, but slowly, he raised his pistol with trembling arm, pointed it at his own eye and pulled the trigger.

Oblonsky smiled. A truly dreadful sight to behold. There had been no real reason for him to glamor the guard into committing suicide. He could have just knocked him out, or glamoured him into going back to the guardhouse and sitting there for a few hours. But this was much more amusing. Almost hilariously so. Making someone shoot themselves in the eye.

Tres droll.

However, it was nothing compared to what he was going to do to the cowardly, pant-soiling so-called detective when this was over.

They strolled down the driveway; the lamps dotted along the sweeping entrance lighting them intermittently as they walked between the pools of light. The detective noticed that whenever the two vampires were in the shadows, they disappeared from sight. Ghostly apparitions as opposed to solid flesh.

Gunter saw guards on the roof rushing to cover them, rifles pointed in their direction. The two human mercenaries took a knee and brought their rifles to bear. There was a flurry of shots and the rooftop guards pinwheeled backwards as the devastatingly accurate fire slammed into them.

The two vampire monsters continued walking as calmly as if they were strolling down an office corridor. Gunter scuttled behind them, his shoulders hunched, his rectum puckering up in anticipation of being shot.

The front door opened and a crowd of armed guards sprinted out. Gunter fell to the floor, but Oblonsky leaned down, grabbed him by the collar, hauled him up and dragged him towards the door.

The mercenaries peppered the guards with well-aimed suppressing fire, keeping their heads down.

And then the second vampire. The one whose name Gunter did not know, blurred into motion, covering the twenty yards between him and the guards almost instantaneously.

The resulting carnage was like someone had thrown a body into a woodchipper. Never had Gunter seen such wanton violence. The vampires didn't just kill – they maimed and dismembered and tore asunder. And they laughed while they did so. After it was all over, they lapped at the pooled blood like dogs.

Gunter gagged and then threw up.

That was merely the beginning.

By the time they had cleared the mansion, Gunter had nothing left in his stomach.

And sitting opposite him, staring up at the two monster vampires, was Hamburg's most notorious criminal.

Die Kettensage.

Gunter had to admit, the gangster showed no

signs of fear. Not even a flicker, despite the fact that two of the most terrifying beings he had ever seen were staring at him the way a dog stares at a portion of prime rib.

'*Du widerlich hässliches tier,*' sneered the Chainsaw.

Oblonsky smiled. 'You call me an ugly animal?' then he shrugged, massively muscled shoulders shifting like tectonic plates. 'Actually, you may be correct. I am undeniably ugly. An animal? Maybe that as well. But at least I am not about to die in the most horrifically painful way imaginable.'

And for the first time an expression of unease wavered across the Chainsaw's face.

'We have come for The *Triginta Argenteous,*' stated Oblonsky.

The Chainsaw looked puzzled. 'I don't know what that is,' he snapped. 'And even if I did, I wouldn't tell you. In fact...'

Before he could continue, Oblonsky blurred forward and casually ripped the Chainsaw's ring finger off his right hand. But he didn't stop there. He continued, like he was plucking a bouquet for a loved one. Two, three, four fingers and a thumb joined the first digit.

The gangster gaped at his ruined appendage and then he opened his mouth as wide as he could – and screamed.

Oblonsky backhanded him, smashing his teeth out and splitting his lips. Then he casually plucked off his ears and dropped them on the floor to join his fingers.

The second vampire chuckled softly. The scene was amusing, but not so amusing as to warrant full blown laughter.

'I swear,' sobbed the Chainsaw through his ruined mouth, his bluster and bravado now nonexistent. 'I don't know what you are talking about.'

'I believe you,' responded Oblonsky. 'So now I shall explain. A necklace, made up of a series of silver Roman Denarias circa 33 AD.'

'Yes, yes,' slobbered the gangster. 'In my saferoom. I have it.'

'The code to get into the room,' said Oblonsky.

'It's my birth date.'

Oblonsky flicked the gangster on the nose, the seemingly ineffectual gesture shattered his nose and almost ripped it from his face, the severed flesh and cartilage hanging obscenely from his cheek.

This time the second vampire burst out laughing.

Oblonsky grinned at him.

'Is very funny,' said the second vamp in a strong Russian accent. 'Like Picasso painting. You are true artist.'

'How the hell would I know what your birth date is, you worthless piece of *dermo*?'

'08111962' blubbed the Chainsaw.

Oblonsky turned to Gunter. 'Do you know

where the saferoom is?'

Gunter nodded. 'I have studied the blueprints. It's on the floor above.'

'Right,' the monster grabbed The Chainsaw by his hair and picked him up. 'Lead us there. Let us see if this rubbish is telling the truth.'

They stopped outside the saferoom. Oblonsky punched the code into the keypad at the side of the door. There was a hiss of hydraulics and the massive steel door swung open.

'It is in there?' he asked the gangster.

'Yes. Please don't hurt me anymore.'

'Just a little,' replied the monster.

And he tilted the man's head to one side, exposing his neck. Then, with a shrill cry of glee, he bit down, ravening and sucking on the gangster's life's blood.

Finally, after he had his fill, he dropped the broken corpse to the floor and strode into the room, blood and gore dripping from his lips and teeth.

'Where is it?' he asked Gunter.

'I don't know.'

'Find it. Now.'

Gunter staggered around the room, checking the various exhibits. Eventually he stopped next to a glass case, studied the object for a few seconds and then opened the case and held up the item.

'Here,' he said. 'I think this is it.'

Oblonsky walked over.

craig zerf

Gunter was holding up a silver necklace. Hanging from it was a single Roman Denaria.

'Where is the rest of it?' asked Oblonsky. 'There are meant to be thirty pieces.'

Gunter shrugged. 'I don't know,' he admitted. 'Maybe it's been split up. Maybe this isn't it. After all, I didn't have a lot of information to go on. This is the best I could do.'

Oblonsky took the pendant from the detective. He looked closely at it. There was no denying – it was an object of serious power. He could feel the waves of influence coming off it like heat from a blast furnace.

'This is part of it,' he announced. 'I can feel its presence.'

'So, I have done well,' ventured Gunter, unable to keep the obvious relief from his voice.

Oblonsky shook his head, causing the tumors and wattles of flesh to shiver and bounce. 'No,' he said. 'We tasked you with finding the entire thing. Not one thirtieth of it.'

He grasped Gunter's face in his huge right hand and slowly, ever so slowly, squeezed.

Until, with an audible pop, the detective's brains exploded out of his ears.

And this time the second vampire could hardly contain his mirth.

CHAPTER 38

The hunters decided to drive to the town of Sonne just outside of Genoa where one of Smirnov's holding houses were situated. They could have flown, but as the drive was only around nine hours, Emily figured by the time they had chartered a plane, booked in, driven to the airport and then organized transport after landing, it was simpler to just take the Globetrotter Motorhome with its armor, run flat tires and fully stocked gunroom.

'It can't have been the Morrigan,' said Troy. 'Merlin and the Prof exiled her.'

Muller snorted. 'Is that what you call it? They imprisoned her in some sort of eternal dungeon, forcing her to relive her most dreaded thoughts and memories over and over for all eternity.'

'Whatever,' said Troy. 'Harsh, but she deserved it. My point is, it couldn't have been her.'

'It was,' responded Emily. 'Not sure how, or why, but it was her.'

'Don't worry none, baby girl,' said Tag, speaking from the driver's seat. 'Ain't nothing we can do about it, so put it on the backburner for now.

Let's concentrate on the things we got some control over. Like making these people-butchers regret they ever lived.'

Emily nodded.

They stopped at a service station to fill up with diesel and to have a sit-down lunch.

Em marveled at the food on offer in what was ostensibly a roadside gas station. The French would never stoop to serving fast food and stale sandwiches. Instead, they perused a small menu that included dishes like *Duck al orange*, *Bouef Bourguignon*, *moules mariniere* and *cassolette*.

Tag frowned at the menu like it was personally trying to offend him. Finally, he asked. 'Don't they just do a burger? With cheese? And fries?'

'Have the *Bouef Bourguignon*,' said Emily.

'Want a burger.'

'It's beef stew,' continued Emily. 'We can all have it.'

Tag raised an eyebrow. 'I like stew.'

'Cool.' Emily ordered for all of them, speaking in fluent French.

The waiter returned quickly with four steaming bowls of stew, a large carafe of water, glasses and a basket of bread.

The *Bourguignon* was spectacular.

Four hours later they were driving through the outskirts of Genoa, following Emily's directions to a hotel she had booked earlier that day.

'We'll freshen up and then do a recce on the slave place,' she said when they arrived and booked in.

The rest of the team mumbled their agreement.

'I hope this place serves French stew,' added Tag. 'It's my new favorite meal.'

CHAPTER 39

Jebe had never seen the Blood King so angry. Usually, he was the very soul of measured response. But for some reason, the item Oblonsky handed over had driven Belikov into an apoplectic rage.

Maksim Sidorov, the vampire who had accompanied Oblonsky to Hamburg went down on one knee. 'My king,' he said, head held low. 'At least this is a start. A beginning. We have the first part of the *Triginta*.'

Both Jebe and Oblonsky took a few steps back, physically divorcing themselves from the kneeling Adept, expressions of absolute disbelief on their faces. Incredulous that a mere Adept had dared to even speak uninvited in front of the *Tsar*.

But Sidorov knew what he was doing. And he knew the risk he was taking. But he was a vampire with ambition. He strove to gain influence in the house, and he knew the only way to do so was to bring himself to the King's attention. To make himself as invaluable as possible.

'If I might dare, Great King,' continued

Sidorov. 'Place me in charge of finding the treasure. I will bend myself entirely to doing so. No stone shall be left unturned and nothing will stand in my way. This I swear.'

Belikov stopped mid rant and stared at the kneeling vamp. Then he smiled. 'You hear that, Jebe?' he asked. 'A follower with some balls. Keen to show his worth to his King.'

Jebe said nothing. He had known Belikov for many hundreds of years and had seen him in this frame of mind before. The best thing to do was nothing. Be still. Don't move. And most importantly, do not speak unless told to.

The monster King stroked Sidorov's head, running his hand over the vampire's growths and tumors. A loving father.

'So,' he said softly. 'You would like to be in charge?'

The Adept nodded.

'Instead of Jebe? The brother I have known and trusted for a thousand years. What do you think, Jebe?' Belikov addressed his second in command. 'Is this member of my house ready to lead.'

Jebe still didn't answer. The decades had long schooled him as to when the Blood King was asking a question rhetorically or literally.

Sidorov, however, had not had his years of experience and, as a result, decided to make an impact. 'I assure you, my King,' he said. 'I am ready.'

Belikov's hand had not left Sidorov's head yet

as the Blood King continued to pet him like a faithful dog. Then, in a blur of motion, the Blood King dropped his hand and forced his fingers into the kneeling vampire's mouth, smashing his front teeth as he did so.

Then, with a savage jerk, he pushed down, tearing Sidorov's bottom jaw off his face. The Adept shrieked wordlessly, the sound coming out more high-pitched gurgle than scream, due to the lack of lower mandibles.

Belikov's knee came up hard and fast, connecting with the ruined remains of Sidorov's face with enough force to shatter the rest of the bones in his skull. Then the King picked him up and threw him towards Jebe.

'Finish this arrogant piece of crap,' he commanded.

Jebe grabbed the mewling vampire by the back of his skull, wrapped another hand around his neck, and with a shrug of his shoulders, plucked the remains of his head off like he was picking a ripe strawberry.

Oblonsky did his best to hide his smirk. This was truly amusing, but he knew better than to look like he may be laughing at the Blood King. So, he quickly changed his smirk into a sneer aimed at the broken corpse of the former Adept with aspirations.

Belikov turned, walked over to his desk, sat down and picked up the necklace. Then he gestured towards Jebe. 'Sit, friend. And you, Oblonsky, wipe that smirk off your ugly face and clean this place up.'

Oblonsky bowed deeply and saw to removing the body and fetching a familiar to mop up the pools of blood.

'What do you think of this?' asked Belikov as he pushed the necklace across the desk to his friend.

Jebe picked it up and studied it closely. 'It has power,' he answered. 'Immense power. I have no doubt it is a part of the *Triginta.* However, finding it raises more questions than answers. Where are the rest of the coins? How does it work? Can we progress with just this one coin?'

'Good questions all,' admitted Belikov. 'Who do we have that possess knowledge about arcane items? And I'm not talking about those idiots we have working on the problem at the moment. All of those minds, all of those years of experience, and together they have unearthed almost nothing of value.'

'The Ancient, *Faylsuf* Ali Hadad,' answered Jebe instantly.

'Ah, yes. The Arab professor.'

Jebe smiled. 'Philosopher, actually, my King. That is what the *Faylsuf* indicates. And to be honest, he prefers to be referred to as a Thamudian, not an Arab.'

'Frankly, I don't care.'

'Nor should you, my King,' concurred Jebe. 'But he is a crusty old scholar and, dare I say, shows little respect where it is due. Also, he has no fear. Literally, I believe the condition is known as Urbach-Wiether syndrome. So, threats do little to motivate him. He is purely driven by his thirst for knowledge. And blood, of course.

'The only reason I have not used him yet is, honestly, because he is so difficult to deal with. I suspect he is more than a little insane.'

'Summon him.'

'As you command, my Tsar.'

CHAPTER 40

The target building was very similar to the one the hunters had hit before. It seemed that Smirnov had expanded his people trafficking business like a MacDonald's, keeping each holding warehouse and layout the same. Fast food for vampires.

A quick recce showed this urban prison was almost empty. Troy reported he could smell five guards but no prisoners.

Emily cussed under her breath.

'Hey, that's good there's no prisoners here,' said Tag.

'Maybe,' answered Emily. 'But it could also mean we just missed them. Maybe they sent them off to the vamps yesterday. We should have hit the place as soon as we arrived.'

Troy shook his head. 'No,' he stated. 'The residual smells are days old. The last time they held anyone here was most likely four days ago. Nothing we could have done would have made any difference.'

Em didn't say anything, but they could see by the set of her shoulders, she was a little happier that their inadvertent tardiness had not resulted in the death of the very people they were trying to save.

'Five of them,' said Emily. 'Okay, guys, don't kill them. Not straight away at any rate. We need to question them. The more we can find out about this setup the better. We need to cleanse this organization from the face of the earth. I want no building, no vehicle, no personnel left. No way for anyone else to restart the operation. I know that Smirnov answered all we asked him, but as we know, information is power, and you can never have too much of it. So, interrogate, then kill.'

The rest of the team nodded.

They didn't get fancy. In fact, they didn't have a plan beyond, kick the front door down, walk in, grab occupants, question them.

'Split up,' said Emily as Tag breached the front door. 'As soon as you have subdued anyone you come across, bring them back here to the entrance lobby. Go.'

Troy went left, Muller went right, and Tag and Emily strode deeper into the building. As soon as they reached the next point of divergence, Emily sent Tag off on his own.

A couple of shots rang out, followed by the dull thump of fists striking human flesh.

One scream cut short.

Emily smiled and then proceeded to her chosen target.

Ten minutes later she stood in the entrance once again, sitting at her feet, a large man sporting two black eyes and a bleeding lip.

Then Troy appeared with two unconscious guards, one slung over each shoulder. He dumped them unceremoniously at Emily's feet, next to her prisoner.

Muller arrived next, dragging his captive by the hair. The man squealed at every step the Knight took. Muller cuffed him on the head and slung him next to the other three.

A few seconds later, Tag entered. He was dragging his captive by his arm.

Emily took one look at the captive's misshapen face and knew straight away there was no chance he was still alive.

'Tag,' she snapped. 'I thought I said, alive.'

The big man looked down at the body and assumed an expression of over-the-top surprise. 'Oh no,' he exclaimed. 'How did that happen?'

Emily bent down and took a closer look at the dead man's face.

'Tag, you hit him so hard you crushed his skull. Then it looks like you tried to squish it back into shape so we wouldn't notice.'

The big man scuffed his feet and looked away.

Emily put her hands on her hips.

'Okay,' said Tag. 'My bad. He took a shot at me and so I had to explain nicely to him that it was rude, and the next thing he was all, like, sort of head caved in. Maybe his skull has some sort of defect. Brittle bone disease or something.'

Both Troy and Muller set their faces, struggling not to laugh at the big man's discomfort.

Emily sighed. 'Oh well, I suppose four out of five isn't that bad.'

Tag smiled, happy that he was no longer in trouble.

Emily grabbed the captive closest to her by the neck and held him up. 'Right,' she said, her eyes glowing red. 'Question time.'

CHAPTER 41

As they drove off, the sound of fire engine sirens got closer.

Muller called the fire department a few minutes after Tag had dropped a batch of thermite grenades into the warehouse. As was their usual *modus operandi*, they set fire to the building with the bodies inside.

'Man, I thought those dudes would never stop talking,' said Tag. 'Girly, you got a way with threats. Hell, one even started to give you his first-grade teacher's name and number.'

Emily frowned. She hated questioning people. Even though they were undeniably the scum of the earth, it felt too close to bullying. Let alone the fact they usually ended up dead.

But that was her calling. Death and retribution. Shadowhunters protected the innocent from the evils they didn't even know existed. And that left no room for her personal feelings.

No parades and medals and public approbation for her and her team.

Just battle, and loss and the knowledge that you were doing good.

The darkness welled up inside her once again, threatening to overwhelm her humanity with its need for power. It's dreams of control. It whispered to her always, even in her sleep.

You could be queen. They are but sheep. They need a leader.

They are below you.

They are worthless.

You are all powerful.

Troy put his arm around her and pulled her towards him, enveloping her with his muscular arms, his warmth, his scent.

His inherent goodness and caring.

He kissed her softly and, for a while again, everything was alright. She was not alone.

Muller was driving, and as he followed the Satnav directions on his cell, he wondered if the next step was one too far. Emily had gotten each guard's home address out of them and now they were proceeding to the closest residence. The young Shadowhunter had commanded they search it and then destroy it. Muller had argued that burning the houses down would expose them to the unnecessary risk of butting heads with local law enforcement. Also, innocents could be harmed if the fires got out of control. There could be collateral damage.

But Emily had not concurred. They would alert the fire departments in a timely fashion, she said. And the law would never find them. Not with the skills of evasion the team possessed.

Muller had agreed. But it bothered him. He knew this was total war. But burning down houses did not sit well with him. It smacked of mere destruction more than retribution. Wanton vandalism as opposed to punishment.

But he was part of the team. And the rest of the team agreed, so he would comply.

The directions took them to a middle-class neighborhood. Well maintained houses. Late model sedans. Children's bicycles outside some front doors.

Muller pulled up outside their destination. The house looked the same as all of the others, bar the fact it was a little less well groomed. The small front lawn needed a trim. The flower beds needed weeding and a coat of paint would not have gone amiss.

There were no signs of life.

'No need for us all to go in,' said Em. 'Tag, you and Troy take a look. Check if there's a study or a desk with any interesting papers in it. Bank details would be good. If he's been paid via bank transfer, then we can check if Smirnov actually did spill all regarding his bank accounts. Then we'll see about draining them so no one else can benefit from his ill begotten gains. After that, place a couple of thermite grenades and we'll call the fire department. They'll get here in time to contain the blaze so the house will be a write off, but the neighbors will be okay.'

'You got it,' responded Tag. 'What if we find

anyone in the house? You know, maid, partner?'

Emily hesitated before she answered. 'Umm – look, if they attack you, respond in kind. If not, disable them and bring them out. Dump them on the front lawn far enough away so they're safe.'

Both Troy and Tag nodded.

Muller took a deep breath, but said nothing. This was the sort of situation that could lead to inadvertent collateral damage, and it made him uncomfortable. The risk did not equal the re- ward as far as he was concerned.

A mere twenty minutes later, Tag and Troy re- turned.

Muller phoned the fire department and gave them the address, reporting there was a fire, then he drove off, heading to the next residence.

'That was quick,' said Emily.

Troy shrugged. 'Not much of interest. Looked like he hardly stayed there. Barely anything in the fridge, no crockery, no pictures or photos. Definitely no study or desk. So, we torched the place and came straight out.'

'There was this,' added Tag. Putting a cell and an address book down on the table between the chairs.

'Maybe he used Apple Pay on his cell,' said Emily. 'If he's like most people, he'll have his passwords in the address book. I'll take a look, see if I can get into his bank through that.'

'You can hack stuff?' asked Tag.

Emily grinned and tapped the side of her head.

'I think so. Remember, I retain everything I've ever read or seen. Everything. I've just got to give it a go, and if the knowledge is there, it'll surface.'

'Awesome,' said the big man.

Troy scoffed. 'Not so much,' her said. 'You ever try to argue with someone who remembers every word you ever said? Verbatim.'

'Can't say that I have,' admitted Tag.

'I don't recommend it,' advised Troy.

'We're here,' stated Muller as he pulled the vehicle to the side of the road.

Another middle-class suburb. The houses and gardens slightly larger. More trees.

'That's the house,' said the Knight, pointing at a white, stucco bungalow.

'Right, Muller, you and Tag take this one,' commanded Emily.

Muller nodded and he and the big man debussed and strode towards the front door.

'What the hell is he doing?' snapped Em. 'I told them to recce first, not to simply walk up and knock on the door like some traveling salesman.'

'Hey, it's Muller, he marches to the beat of his own drum,' said Troy. 'Anyway, there's nothing to worry about, no normal human being could harm him and Tag. They're a force of nature.'

'That's not the point,' said Em. 'I told them what to do and they simply ignored me.'

Troy frowned but said nothing, he could tell

that Emily was freaking out over the whole people trafficking thing. And rightly so, it was a heinous crime that needed to be stopped. But he couldn't help but feel she might be pushing things a bit too far with her current scorched earth policy.

He watched as Muller knocked on the front door. The door opened and Troy could see the Knight conversing with someone. Then he nodded, the door shut and he and Tag walked back to the vehicle and got back in.

'What was that all about?' asked Emily.

'That was the gangster's wife,' answered Muller. 'And his kid. Young boy, maybe six or seven.'

'And?'

'And there is no way I'm going to burn their house down.'

There was an uncomfortable silence for a few seconds and then Emily spoke.

'Thank you, Muller,' she said softly. 'You're right, of course.' The young Shadowhunter paused, collecting her thoughts. 'You know, before, when we were all last together, we had Merlin, and William to lead us. Now, for some reason, I seem to have become the leader. Not sure how that happened, to be honest. So, what I'm trying to say is, maybe you should take the reins. Or Troy, after all he is the Omega.'

'What about me?' asked Tag.

'Or you,' conceded Emily.

Tag chuckled. 'No way, baby girl,' he said. 'Just

pulling your leg. Tag doesn't want to lead anyone. I be the strong silent type, not the tell-you-what-to-do type. Tall dark and handsome, that's my remit. Anyway, if we voting, you get my vote.'

'Me too,' echoed Troy.

They all turned to face Muller.

The Knight spun the ignition and revved the engine to life before he spoke. 'You lead,' he said. 'I will follow. But do not ask me to do anything my church would not agree with. And that includes making innocent people homeless.'

'Okay,' conceded Emily. 'I shall rely on you to be my conscience.'

'No,' replied Muller. 'You must be your own conscience, control your own morality. But I will always be here to guide, to lean on and to listen. Deal?'

'Deal.' Concurred Emily.

'That's my man,' said Tag. 'Muller the Pious. Knight extraordinaire. Hi five, holy man.'

Muller didn't even take his eyes off the road. 'No.'

Tag chuckled. 'Fair enough, you drive, I'll high five myself.'

'Where to now?' asked Muller.

'Hotel,' replied Emily. 'As those ass wipes told us, they got places at Lyon and outside of Paris we need to shut down. I say we pick up our baggage and drive through the night. I don't want to take the chance of them shipping any prisoners

199

out before we get there. Particularly as by now I'm sure they know that Smirnov is no more.'

All murmured their agreement.

CHAPTER 42

'*Faylsuf* Ali Hadad,' said Belikov. 'Now you are here, I recall. We have met before.'

'On numerous occasions, Blood King,' confirmed the philosopher. 'But it was long ago, before the … umm … Chernobyl event. Obviously, I look a little different now, since the meltdown.'

'But your aura remains the same,' noted the Blood King. 'Where was it, the Holy City?'

'And after, when I was traveling with the Knights Templar. But I have been living in your residence for many years now. We simply have not run into each other.'

'Ah yes, I remember it all well,' affirmed Belikov. 'The infamous Arab who fought for the infidels.'

'Thamudian, not Arab.'

'Whatever.'

'No, *Krov Tsar*, not whatever, how would you like it if I referred to you as a Caucasian?'

'I would think nothing of it, because you wouldn't dare to refer to a pure-bred Russian as *Chernozhopy*.'

'But if I did?'

'Enough,' roared Belikov. 'I will call you whatever I want. Learn your place, Arab.'

Hadad turned and walked away, heading for the door.

'Halt this instant,' commanded the King.

'Certainly not,' replied the philosopher. 'Find someone else to insult. But if you are looking for an intellect that even approaches mine, well, good luck with that, Blood King.'

Belikov glanced at Jebe and gestured with a mere nod of his head.

Jebe flashed across the room and dragged the philosopher back to stand before his king.

The two monster vampires stared at each other. The philosopher and the king.

'Are you always this obtuse, Thamudian?' asked Belikov.

Hadad gave the king's question some serious thought. As always, he never answered without applying himself fully to the question in hand. Finally, he nodded. 'Yes, my king,' he said. 'I believe so.'

Belikov stared for a while and then a rumble started in his chest and, after a few seconds, rang out across the room. 'So be it,' he said through his laughter. 'You are now my official advisor, second only to myself and Jebe. Sit down, my Thamudian philosopher, I have some questions for you.'

CHAPTER 43

The team drove through the night, taking turns to sleep while they traveled. The trip took just under eight hours and they arrived on the outskirts of Lyon as the sun was rising.

Unlike the others, Emily had not slept at all. Instead, she spent the night working on hacking into Smirnov's bank accounts using the minimal information she had available to her.

Fortunately, her sky-high IQ plus her eidetic memory allowed her to achieve in a mere six hours what most people would take weeks to do.

'You spend all night looking at that screen?' asked Troy as he lit a morning cigarette.

Em smiled and nodded.

'How did it go?'

'Victory,' she said with a chuckle. 'I haven't managed to track down and clean out everything, but I'm pretty sure I've hit his bigger accounts and drained them. Over three million dollars. I'll see the money goes to the victims and their families. It's not much, but it's a start.

'Whatever happens, I reckon we can safely say

craig zerf

Smirnov's evil enterprise will not last much longer without leadership or funds.'

'Yeah,' agreed Tag. 'Or without anyone alive to staff it.'

'The thing that is still bothering me,' said Muller from the driver's seat. 'Is how one supplier got together with all of the different *Nosferatu* houses. And a Russian one at that. It smacks of cooperation and that's bad.'

'Look, Muller,' replied Emily. 'You're right. We have to look into this whole Russian conspiracy theory of yours, and we will. As soon as we've wrapped up Smirnov's operation.'

'It's all connected,' interjected the Knight. 'Smirnov, the Russian *Nosferatu*, those pig-ugly monster vamps we fought. I'm telling you, Emily, I'm not simply raving, I'm really nervous. This is the harbinger of serious things to come. Earth shattering, world ending stuff. I can feel it in my bones.'

No one spoke for a while as Muller's dire predictions sunk in. They had all spoken about it before, but the Knight's obvious concern was getting to them.

'Anyway,' added Muller. 'We're here. Plan of action, boss.'

Em frowned, not sure if Muller was joshing her or not by calling her, boss. 'Same old,' she answered. 'Tag and you take the front; Troy and I will take the back. Keep some alive, check for prisoners. You know the drill.'

'And hope none of those ugly dudes are in residence,' added Tag.

'Amen to that,' concurred Muller as he got out of the vehicle.

A mere twenty minutes later the team met in the lobby at the front of the warehouse. It is not possible for an attack on a group of armed people to become mundane, as danger always lurks in the most unexpected places, but in so much as it could, the process had become rather pedestrian.

The five miscreants knelt in a row in front of Emily. Although, to be fair, one of them had to be leaned against the wall lest he fall over.

Tag stood next to Emily, a beaming smile on his face.

'Hey, check it out,' he said as he gestured at the almost unconscious captive. 'Punched the dude, knocked him out – and didn't kill him.'

Emily rolled her eyes. 'Well done, Tag,' she said. After all, praise deserved should be praise given.

But as she spoke, the man in question threw up and then fell sideways, his entire body shaking and twitching as he began to fit. Seconds later, his back arched and, with a final grunt, he went slack.

Troy knelt next to him and laid a finger in his neck. Then he shook his head. 'He's gone.'

'Not my fault,' said Tag. 'You all saw. He was fine until a few seconds ago. Must be some genetic thing. I've heard of this before. SDS. Sudden Death Syndrome. Dudes just expire for no apparent reason. Just my luck,' he continued. 'The one I bring in is an SDS sufferer. Oh well, never mind, still got a whole bunch left.'

The four surviving captives stared at the big man like he was barking mad, the looks of fear on the faces blatantly apparent.

'Please,' stammered the one. 'Who are you? I don't understand what we've done wrong?'

'Seriously?' asked Emily. 'How about kidnapping innocent people and selling them to vampires as food? That do for a start?'

The man looked at Emily as if she had gone insane.

'Vampires? WTF? There's no such thing.'

Emily sighed. Then she leaned forward and let the Daywalker out. Her canines lengthened, her eyes glowed bright red and a wave of power pulsed over the captives like a tsunami of terror.

One of the captives passed out, two started to scream and the one talking to Emily began to shake like he had been in a freezer for a few hours.

'We didn't know,' he said, his voice a whining plea for clemency.

'What did you think you were kidnapping them for?' asked Emily.

The man shrugged. 'I dunno. Hookers? Sex slaves? Not food.'

'Oh, sex slaves, so that makes it alright, does

it?'

The man stared. He knew that any answer he gave would most likely lead to pain. So, he decided to stay silent.

Emily shook her head. Then she turned to Muller. 'I can't stay in the room with this scum,' she said. 'Lest I kill them all before we question them. Can you do it?'

The Knight nodded,

'Thank you,' said Emily as she left the room, reverting to her fully human form as she did.

Troy started to follow her but she shook her head. 'I need a bit of time alone,' she said. 'If that's okay with you.'

Troy nodded and stood back.

As Emily left the building her super-hearing picked up the sound of bone meeting flesh. A solid, wet thud.

Then she heard Muller sigh. 'Tag, come on, why did you just smash that guy's head in?'

'Because he upset the girly,' rumbled Tag. 'Don't fret, holy man, you still got three more.'

Emily smiled. She knew she shouldn't. Smashing someone brains out with your bare fist wasn't actually something to grin about, but sometimes Tag's obvious care for her made her happy, no matter how heavy handed it was.

CHAPTER 44

Hadad was in his element, surrounded by ancient tomes, computer on his desk, unrestricted access to anyone he wanted to talk to and unlimited funds.

Truth be told, before the Blood King had approached him about the *Triginta Argenteous*, the thousand-year-old philosopher had been bored. He loved knowledge, hungered after it, but after ten centuries, he found little that still excited him.

The story of Judas Iscariot had always fascinated Hadad. He couldn't think of a more spectacular fall from grace in the lexicons of history. To have been chosen above so many, offered the keys to a kingdom, and then to betray all for what would translate to less than $1000 in today's money.

Modern theories dictate that Iscariot then tried to return the blood money, and when the gesture was refused, he flung the money into the temple and went off to hang himself.

Hadad knew this wasn't the complete truth. In fact, he did attempt to return the money, but when it was refused, he did not try to hang himself. Instead, he simply left. And according to many of the reports Hadad could find, Judas clung onto his silver. Like a talisman. Even in his most destitute moments he never spent it. It was all he had to remind him of his Lord, and of what he had done.

He never forgave himself.

But what he discovered over time was that the Thirty Pieces of silver had been imbued with a power. He found he had traded his humanity for more than simple metal. The coins themselves had been imbued with the power of the Disciples. They called out for followers.

At first, he thought he had been forgiven. Blessed with the powers of leadership. Destined to have a band of followers.

And then he found it was quite the opposite. Because, although he attracted cohorts, they were always the very worst of people.

Like attracts like.

He could make no friends with anyone who had even the slightest good in them.

Only the vile. The evil. The corrupt and the venal.

He was being mocked. Belittled.

And over time his remorse turned to hatred.

Hadad tracked Judas's progress across Europe, citing ancient tomes combined with rumor and even a couple of eye witness accounts. The journey the Great Betrayer had taken was most interesting. Notably the change from remorseful ex-disciple, to callous thief and murderer.

He continued to roam, unable to put roots down anywhere as he was plagued constantly by hatred and mistrust, no matter what he did.

After many years he met an ancient vampire Master, Augustus Sextus. An ex-*Tribunus* in the Roman army. They became friends, as the vampire was the first being Iscariot had met since his downfall that approached his own level of evil.

The Master willingly turned the Great Betrayer into a *Nosferatu*, hoping for a true friend and ally.

However, once again Iscariot's base nature combined with the Power of the *Triginta* came to the fore, and instead of following Sextus, Judas slayed him. Removing his head and stealing all he could carry.

Again, he disappeared for many years only to surface during the Germanic tribal wars.

It was here where the Great Betrayer finally had his miserable life ended. Killed in a scuffle by a minor chieftain, Euric son of Theodoric.

Euric relieved Judas of his thirty pieces of silver, and was so enamored by the silver coins that he had them fashioned into a necklace.

He wore it constantly from that day forward.

The power of the *Triginta* helped Euric unite the Visigoth hordes, become king, crush the Romans and go on to control most of Europe.

Until, in short time, the curse of the *Triginta*

showed itself and Euric died a painful death by 'Natural Causes'. Taken to his grave by a series of flesh rotting tumors.

And after that, Hadad could find no more trace of the *Triginta*.

Had it been buried with the king? If so, how did one piece of it end up in a German gangster's private collection? Where was the rest of it?

The logical place to start looking would be the grave of King Euric. The only problem being, no one knew exactly where the grave was. Most likely somewhere in, or near, Toulouse. Not quite a needle in a haystack, but very close. And Hadad couldn't do any field work. Apart from the fact he could only venture out at night, he was hideously deformed from the radiation poisoning, so there was no way he could pass himself off as anything but what he was.

A monster.

Instead, he knew exactly who, or what, he could call on. If the truculent, self-absorbed SOB would deign to help. Which was unlikely.

Nevertheless, Hadad had to try.

First, he had to make contact. For this he needed a stone bowl, two pints of fresh human blood, and a mirror made from polished brass.

Getting up out of his chair he rifled through one of his chests and, after a minute, pulled out a stone bowl. A short while later he found the brass mirror.

Then he rang a bell.

Within moments a familiar knocked and entered.

The philosopher handed him the bowl.

'Get this filled to the brim with fresh blood,' he commanded. 'It matters not whom it comes from, use any of the food. Hurry.'

The familiar bowed and scuttled off.

Less than an hour later, Hadad placed the bowl on his desk and propped the mirror behind it at such an angle it reflected the surface of the blood. Then he sprinkled a pinch of dried herbs into the bowl, muttered an arcane chant and waited.

The spell was powerful, but it took a while to work.

The evening moved on. However, Hadad did not. In order for the scrying bowl to connect, he needed to continually feed a dribble of power into it. So, it needed his constant attention.

It would have been much easier if he could have simply used a cell to make contact. But that would never work. The problem with cellular communication is that it is unable to connect with the Fae world. Different continents are fine, but different planes of existence – not so much.

Because the being Hadad was attempting to contact was none other than Arend Redwurm.

And Arend was a *Hulder*.

Modern vernacular had changed how people now referred to his race, and frivolous fantasy fiction had further corrupted both his people's history and their perceived demeanor.

Nowadays, Arend would be referred to as an Elf. And visions of Legolas and Lord of the Rings would spring to mind.

Nothing could be further from the truth. Although, to be fair, some of the modern perceptions and beliefs held water.

Hulders were incredibly long-lived. They *were* graceful, tall and seemingly emotionless. They also happened to be exceptional warriors.

But they were not fair of hair and skin. Nor were they pinup, heart throb pretty.

Their features were uncomfortably angular and their skin was closer to blue-gray than Hitler youth. Eyes were like polished coals in their head. Two orbs of shiny obsidian. Although mere humans would be unable to see their true visage unless the *Hulder* wanted it so. Instead, they would see what they wanted to see. A tall, attractive human being. Such was the natural power of the *Hulder's* glamor.

And there were no similes that came close to describing the depth of their absolute narcissism. Not for nothing was there a popular saying amongst the Fae, reserved for only the most arrogant and self-absorbed beings. They were said to be showing, "The Hubris of a *Hulder*".

A crackle of energy rippled across the bloody surface and a scowling face appeared in the brass mirror.

'What?'

'Greetings, Arend Redwurm,' said Hadad. 'I hope I find you well.'

'Get to the point, scholar,' snapped the *Hulder.* 'Time is precious, even for those of us who are gifted with a seeming excess of it.'

'I have a challenge for you,' continued Hadad, knowing the worse thing to do would be to voice his request as a favor.

'You mean you need my help,' corrected Arend. 'Come on, spit it out.'

Hadad contrived to look bored, as if he had already lost interest in involving the Elf. 'Well, we're looking for a certain artifact. Something that involves fieldwork, but if you aren't interested, I can always ask Doctor Cornelius.'

Arend spat over his shoulder in disgust. 'That useless Boggart. That idiot fairy isn't fit to research my skinny *Huldish* ass.'

'Not true,' argued Hadad. 'He's considered to be an expert in the field.'

'What field? What are you looking for?'

The philosopher vampire paused, drawing out his answer. Eventually he sighed, as if it would do him no harm to tell. 'The *Triginta Argenteous*. The Blood King is looking for it. Well, to be exact, he is looking for the rest of it. We already have part of the artifact.'

'You say you have part of it already?' questioned Arend.

Hadad nodded.

'So, it isn't a myth after all.' The Hulder frowned. 'The fabled thirty pieces of silver. Why do you want it?'

'Irrelevant,' answered Hadad. 'Though, what is relevant is what we are prepared to pay for it.'

'I am already wealthy beyond my wildest dreams of avarice,' snapped Arend. 'Do not insult me with tawdry offers of profit.'

'I wouldn't dream of it,' countered Hadad. 'However, what do you know of the Codex du Clos Luca?'

Arend scoffed. 'I know it doesn't exist. It was destroyed in a fire in 1512.'

Hadad, who had been prepared for this moment, picked up a leather bound linen paged book and held it in front of the mirror. 'It seems the rumors of its destruction were a trifle exaggerated.'

Arend did a classic double take. 'Is that real?'

'As real as the Rock of Gibraltar.'

'The full notebooks of Leonardo de Vinci,' breathed the Hulder. 'Where did you find it?'

'Does that matter?'

'No. What would I have to do to see it?'

'If you find the rest of the *Triginta*, the Codex is yours,' offered Hadad.

Tell me what you already know,' said Arend. 'I will commit all of my considerable resources to finding your *Triginta*.'

'Contact me when you have it, and the Codex is yours,' affirmed Hadad.

Arend nodded and broke contact, already keen to start his journey of exploration. Driven by his greed and need for one of the most converted of books amongst those who strive for knowledge above all else.

Hadad smiled. A job well done.

CHAPTER 45

'What do you mean, they are dead?' snapped Belikov.

'Leonid Lebedev and his second, Karl.' Repeated Jebe. 'They have both suffered the true death. And their bodies have been immolated.'

'Impossible.'

Jebe stood still. He didn't answer, because to point out that it patently was possible, as it had just happened, would be an exercise in both futility and stupidity. Unless of course he wanted to join the two dispatched brethren.

'How did it happen?' asked Belikov.

'As you know, my King, I sent the two of them, along with a team of familiars, to protect Smirnov. He claimed that some unknown force was destroying his operation.'

'Belikov waved his hand at Jebe, a gesture that meant, get on with it.

'Long story short, they didn't report back and I was unable to communicate with them. So, after a couple of days, I sent a team of local familiars to investigate. Smirnov's villa was burned to the ground. There were no survivors. Not only that, but two more of his operations have been torched, all of the employees with them. To all intents and purposes, Smirnov's operation no longer exists.'

Neither monster spoke for a while. Belikov deep in thought, Jebe simply waiting.

'I cannot think of any living being besides one of our own House that could defeat both Leonid and Karl in battle,' mused Belikov. 'It would take a company of soldiers, and if a war that size had been waged in a residential area, it would have made the international news.'

Still Jebe refrained from offering thought. He knew if his King wanted him to speak, he would command it.

'Thoughts,' demanded the Tsar.

'What about the rumors?' ventured the second.

Belikov snorted. 'They are just that. Rumors. The possibility of a Daywalker is zero to less than.'

'Yet someone wiped out the United Kingdom and the Italian Houses in one fell swoop,' said Jebe.

'Infighting followed by werewolves. The pack took advantage of the change in power that came about when they started to bicker amongst themselves. When I rule all, pettiness like that shall never happen again. We weaken ourselves by fighting each other like stone aged tribesmen.'

Jebe wondered whether it was worth risking the King's ire and decided it was. After all, he was meant to be Belikov's advisor and only friend.

'There were many corroborated reports, my King,' he insisted. 'Not only of the Daywalker, but also of the Shadowhunter who became a *Nosferatu,* thereby betraying his friends. It was he who tore the houses apart. It is also said that the pack Omega was killed and a new one has risen in his place.'

Belikov breathed heavily for a few seconds. Jebe knew he was doing so to show his displeasure at his second's disagreement. Because neither of them actually had to breathe. They were, after all, undead.

Jebe waited, looking at a spot above his master's head. Avoiding eye contact.

Finally, Belikov spoke. 'I am lucky to have you at my side, friend,' he said softly. 'What you say is true. And it is right to point it out. I deny the existence of the Daywalker because, for the first time in many, many centuries, I feel a twinge of ... fear.'

'They say she is a mere child,' interjected Jebe. 'A slip of a girl.'

'Yet she bested two powerful Houses,' said Belikov.

'She had help.'

'Yes. She did. But if what you suspect is true, she also brought the true death to two of our most respected warriors. Trust me, Jebe, slip of a girl or not, she demands respect. And a healthy dose of fear.' The King chuckled. A dark and sinister sound. 'I like it,' he said. 'It gives one's existence a little spice. What say you, my friend?'

Jeve allowed himself a smile. 'I say, my King has no cause to fear anyone.'

Belikov laughed out loud. 'As always, my friend, you are the consummate diplomat. Whatever, put some people on to tracking these rumors down. I want to know if she exists, where she is and exactly how powerful she is. Then I want her destroyed.'

'You command, my Lord, and so it shall be.'

Jebe bowed and left the room.

CHAPTER 46

It was done. The team of hunters had rooted out every one of Smirnov's setups and destroyed them. Apart from the first raid, they found no more prisoners. But now they knew there would be no further victims. At least not via that particular avenue.

They had also struck a serious blow against the *Nosferatu.* Almost thirty brethren subjected to the true death. Not forgetting those two monsters. The Russian mega-vamps. Or as Tag now referred to them as – the BUMFS (Butt Ugly Mother ... whatever).

Emily booked the team into another five-star Parisian hotel and she retired to Troy's and her room after dinner.

Troy went for a shower and she stood alone on the balcony, staring at the Eiffel Tower, taking in the scents of the city and marveling at the beauty of the French architecture.

Far in the distance she could see the dome of the Notre Dame Cathedral. Her exceptional eyesight allowed her to pick up the multitude of stone Gargoyles. There were over a hundred statues, not all of them gargoyles. Strictly speaking, to be classed as a gargoyle, water had to be channeled through the statue. Otherwise, it was a grotesque. However, for Emily's intents the word gargoyle sufficed. Particularly as that is what they referred to themselves as.

On a whim, she stretched out her senses and opened her mind to communication. Trying once more to communicate with the gargoyles. A rush of random sounds and feelings flooded her senses.

The slow, grinding vibration of Gargoyle communication provided a bass note to the mental cacophony. Over it a babble of French. Human voices.

Then suddenly, without warning, a spike of pain.

Emily dropped to her knees as the pain hammered into her. And with it a voice echoed in her mind.

Spiteful. Malevolent and vindictive.

'*Got you.*'

Emily knew the voice well. She knew now that she had been correct before.

It was the Morrigan.

'Freedom,' she crowed. 'Now I have an anchor to cling to, I can finally get out of this godforsaken prison of insanity that Merlin has banished me to.'

Emily could feel the presence of the warrior women's mind tugging at her. Wrapping itself around her and using her as a pillar on which to pull itself from the foreign plane of existence she was trapped in.

Emily fought back, but she was human. An incredibly enhanced one, to be sure, but still a mere mortal.

And the Morrigan was a god.

Try as she might, Emily could feel the stays of her sanity start to tear free as the Morrigan used the Shadowhunter's mind to enhance her own desperate bid for freedom.

And as Emily felt she had lost the battle, a pure white light appeared in her consciousness. Warm, calming and all powerful.

'Begone, foul woman,' thundered a voice.

Sound and color exploded and Emily found herself floating in a foreverness of blue calm. A warm ocean that supported her in its powerful, welcoming arms. She opened her eyes to find herself lying on her back, still on the balcony.

Above her a familiar face. Long, gray beard. Silver hair, tied back. And violet eyes that spoke of unbelievable authority and wisdom in equal volumes.

'Merlin,' she gasped.

'And in the nick of time it seems,' responded the ancient sorcerer as he picked her up and hugged her close.

Emily glanced over his shoulder to see Troy standing next to the Professor. Both had similar concerned expressions on their faces. The major

craig zerf

difference being that Troy was naked and still wet from running out of his shower when he heard Emily cry out.

'It looks like we need to all sit down so you can tell me what the hell is going on,' said Merlin. 'Are any of the others with you?'

'Tag and Muller,' answered Emily. 'In the hotel.'

Merlin nodded in approval. 'Good,' he turned to Troy. 'Be a good fellow, don some clothing and then go and fetch them, won't you. It's time to caucus.'

CHAPTER 47

Merlin leaned back in his chair, took out his pipe and filled it from a small leather tobacco pouch.

The Professor did the same.

'You should have called me sooner,' said the wizard.

Emily frowned. 'I tried. It's not like I have you on speed dial. You don't even have a cell.'

Merlin raised an eyebrow. 'So instead, you decided it would be a good idea to ask the gargoyles if they could contact me, and you sent out a worldwide distress call set to open all channels?'

'Hey, I'm still new at this,' argued Emily.

'Next time, my child,' said Merlin. 'Simply concentrate on me. Me alone, and call. I will always come. Now,' he continued. 'The way I see it is – we have a load of problems. Let's start at the bottom and work our way up. You have a gang of kidnappers selling innocents to the *Nosferatu* for food. That you appear to have pretty much cleared up. Well done.

'Secondly, you have declared war against the

French and Italian houses. Not altogether a bad thing, after all, it is our job to fight these blood suckers.

'Next, the Russian connection. These monster vampires you have come up against. I know who they are, and let me tell you, this is a big problem. They are part of the House of Belikov. A house of brethren that were affected by the Chernobyl meltdown back in 1986. They have crossed my radar but I never bothered about them because, due to their massive and horrifying deformities, they tended to remain rather reclusive. However, it looks as if the Blood King has developed ambitions above his station. And this is bad. Very bad. By the sounds of things, it appears that Belikov is looking to expand his house and connect with the other European houses. If he does this, we are in big trouble.'

'Won't happen,' interjected the Prof.

'Why?' asked Emily.

'Cats and dogs,' answered the Boggart.

'Meaning?'

'The houses will never unite. Vampires are incredibly territorial. One of the main reasons they have never taken over the world is because they fight like cats and dogs. They are genetically indisposed to forming an alliance.'

'True,' agreed Merlin. 'But you cannot deny this looks like Belikov is trying to do so.'

The Prof frowned. 'Very much so,' he admitted. 'And that in itself is a worry. Especially coming from a vampire as ancient as Belikov. He of all creatures should know it would be impossible to unite the houses. Unless, of course, we are missing something. I shall have to look into this. Yes. Definitely. This is disturbing. I don't like it. No, not at all.'

The Prof harrumphed, stood up and began to pace about the room, talking to himself as he walked.

'Finally,' said Merlin with a puff on his pipe. 'The awakening of the Morrigan.'

'Hey, that wasn't my fault,' said Emily.

'No, it wasn't,' concurred Merlin. 'It was mine. When the Professor and I banished her, I misjudged her power. And her resilience. We can assume that she may have broken free of the plane of imprisonment we trapped her in. Or that at least she might be close.'

The Prof stopped his pacing and pointed his pipe at Merlin. 'Tell them,' he said.

Merlin frowned. 'Later.'

'No,' insisted the Prof. 'Tell them now. They need to know.'

'What are you two talking about?' asked Muller. 'Sounds like something we should know. The Prof is right, information is strength.'

Merlin sighed. 'When we imprisoned the Morrigan, we ... well, it was more than a simple banishment. We looked to punish her for the monstrous things she had done.' Merlin hesitated.

'We all know that. Well, perhaps not exactly

227

how you caried out said punishment, but we know the gist,' said Emily.

'Yes,' breathed the wizard. 'Okay, well, when we locked her away, we did so in a pocket universe. And she was not alone, as such.'

'Meaning?' asked Emily.

'We locked her away with her own nightmares,' explained Merlin. 'With her every fear, her regrets, her failures. Every terrible incident that had ever occurred in her life. And you must remember, the Morrigan is a god. She has been around for countless millennia and has experienced more pain and misery and heartache than a hundred thousand humans put together. Her suffering while locked away must have been – infinite.'

'What the wizard is trying to say,' interjected the Professor. 'Is that our goddess of war might very well have gone completely and utterly insane whilst locked in stasis. Mental.'

'And she will be looking for revenge,' added Merlin. 'Particularly against Emily who, for some reason, she saw as playing a huge part on her downfall.'

'Hey, that crow-lady comes anywhere near the girly, she and Missus Jones are going to have a dance,' said Tag. 'No one harms Emily.'

Troy growled his agreement.

Merlin raised an eyebrow. 'Yes, of course. But let us not forget, the Morrigan is a god. And the god of war, no less. Do not take this lightly.'

'So, what do we do next?' asked Emily.

'We wait,' answered the Prof. 'Until I find out a little more about Belikov and his newfound ambitions. And while Merlin attempts to track down the Morrigan. After all, she may still be entrapped. But even if that is the case, it is no simple task tracking down a folded pocket universe. Particularly if one is looking to keep it secure.'

'Quite,' said Merlin. 'But first, we all get some sleep. Troy, could you phone down to reception and book a pair of rooms for the Professor and I?'

The Omega nodded and walked over to the bedside phone.

Emily went over to Merlin and hugged him again. 'It's good to have you back,' she said.

And the old man smiled.

CHAPTER 48

The air shimmered as a rectangular, door sized light manifested itself in the middle of an empty field. Small arcs of lightning crackled and earthed from the sides of the light, sending up puffs of smoke that caused patches of grass to catch fire.

Then the shimmering coalesced, forming a bright blue, solid panel. Through the panel appeared an arm, then a body followed. Another came after. And another.

When the third body had fully crossed the threshold, the portal winked shut, leaving a burned patch of grass and an overwhelming stink of ozone in the air.

Arend took in a deep breath and smiled. 'I love the smell of ozone in the morning,' he announced. 'Welcome to the realm of the humans,' he continued as he turned to his two companions.

The two beings with him were also *Hulder*. Tall, willowy, grey skinned and sharp featured. One male and one female. Like Arend, they were dressed in fitted leather pants and jackets. They both carried large canvas rucksacks.

Concealed in various sheaths and holsters beneath their jackets were a variety of weapons. Daggers, throwing blades, poisoned darts and even small, spring driven crossbows.

Obviously, all of the blades were obsidian and the metal parts of the weapons were bronze. Steel was an anathema to the Fae.

Arends compatriots, the female, Mist and the male, Remer, were visiting the human realm for the first time. Usually Arend traveled alone, but this time he felt he needed backup. After all, the prize was such that he was bending all to achieve his end goal.

He would find the *Triginta*.

And then the Codex would be his.

The two Fae newcomers looked about, taking in the fields, the trees and the buildings that designated the outskirts of the city of Toulouse in the distance.

Using her farsight, Mist zeroed in on the city. 'Why are their buildings so large?' she asked. 'And so ugly? All squares and sharp angles.'

Arend laughed. 'They are a callow race,' he explained. 'Brutal and warlike. But do not judge too soon. They are also capable of creating items of great beauty. And their scholars are second to none. Despite the fact that they are incredibly short lived, they still manage to accumulate vast oceans of knowledge. Actually, perhaps it is because their lives are so brief they are driven so much more than their Fae counterparts.'

'Is there an inn close by?' asked Remer. 'Or at very least a stable where we can purchase some stout horses?'

Arend grinned, exposing his pointed, yellow teeth. 'I have my own abode near to here,' he replied. 'A short walk. Follow me.'

CHAPTER 49

Both Mist and Remer were bathed in sweat. And their normal blue-gray skin had turned an unhealthy shade of pink.

'Do not fret,' said Arend. 'The runes will take effect soon. Already they are protecting you, just give them another hour or so and you will both feel absolutely fine.'

Mist fingered the crystal that hung from a brass chain around her neck. The surface of the crystal was covered in tiny carved inscriptions. Runes of power.

Arend had provided each of them with the said runed necklaces as they had set off from the portal to get to his abode. They matched one that Arend himself wore around his neck at all times.

'So much iron,' she mumbled, her voice scratchy from nausea. 'It's hideous.'

Arend grinned. The discomfort of his compatriots was highly amusing. 'Rookies,' he thought to himself. 'Complete and utter noobs.'

There were a few reasons he hadn't told them of the preponderance of iron in the human world before they agreed to accompany him. Firstly, they might have refused to come and, secondly, he thought they both needed taking down a peg. Even amongst the *Hulder*, Mist and Remer were considered arrogant. And to be fair, they were entitled to a little conceit. Both were amongst the leading Fae warriors, deadly with bow, blade and empty hand.

But now they were unsettled. And this gave Arend the upper hand. It was typical of him to plan ahead, using every situation to his own advantage. That is how he became one of the wealthiest, most respected scholars in the whole of Faedom. His name was both revered and despised, as it should be. For he was respected and feared in equal measure.

Remer stood up from his chair and, on unsteady legs, rushed to the front door, opened it and threw up violently as his stomach roiled against the vast mass of iron all around him.

Arend took out a long, small bowled clay pipe, filled it with Fae tobacco and, using a small fire spell, lit up. He sat back in his chair and puffed contentedly, the purple smoke rising in the form of perfect smoke rings above his head.

An hour later, he stood up.

'Right,' he said. 'Time's up. The runes will have taken full effect by now. We can move on.'

'I feel like death,' mumbled Remer.

'Mere weakness brought on by the nausea,' said Arend. 'Drink some water. Both of you, quickly now, then come with me.'

The two ill *Hulder* followed his instructions and followed him to the garage.

'Stables?' asked Mist.

'In a manner of speaking,' replied Arend as he pushed the remote, bringing the garage door up to reveal a late model Range Rover in metallic black.

Both of the compatriots stared open eyed.

'Where are the horses?' asked Mist.

Arend thumped the hood. 'Under here.' Then he opened the passenger door, and one of the rear doors. 'Mist, you get in the front. Remer, back.'

The two *Hulder* looked at the steel skinned vehicle in dismay.

'It's an iron box,' stammered Remer in horror. 'We will literally be surrounded by the foul metal.'

Arend pointed at their charmed necklaces. 'Runed against harm,' he said. 'Now get in.'

He opened the driver's door and climbed in, settling himself into the calf-leather seat and putting the keys in the ignition.

He glanced at the two noobs and was pleased to see they had both screwed their courage to the sticking post and, with eyes almost closed from fear, they clambered in, sat down and closed the doors.

Arend turned the ignition. The huge engine rumbled to life and he pulled out of the garage.

Remer let out an involuntary squeak of fear and Mist simply squeezed her eyes tightly shut.

Putting his foot down, Arend gunned the engine and sped towards Toulouse. At the same time, he turned on the radio and opened the Classical channel. Tchaikovsky's 1812 overture boomed out, complete with cannons.

Both compatriots froze. And Arend had to use all of his power to stop himself hooting with laughter.

However, after a few minutes, the two *Hulder* warriors showed their mettle and pulled themselves together.

'Magic?' questioned Remer.

'Internal combustion engine,' answered Arend.

'I don't understand.'

'Obviously. It doesn't matter. It is a physical phenomenon. The humans, on the whole, do not possess magic. They are blind to it.'

'It does not exist here?'

'It does,' answered Arend. 'But only a select few are capable of using it. The rest are blocked by their own narrow minds.'

'And what is this horseless carriage called?' asked Mist.

'It's a motor vehicle,' answered Arend. 'And if you want to blend in here, you are going to have to watch how you talk. No, magic. That and no talking about horseless this and foul iron such what. Tone it down.

'Also, you need to project a glamor. Humans are a rather skittish breed and they do not take well to others that are different to them. Pay attention now, here is how you will need to appear.'

Arend willed an image of a six foot four, blonde, well-built GQ magazine model to appear in his mind. Then he set it free to settle around his physical being, like a second skin.

'Get it?' he asked the two.

They nodded.

'Do it, let me see.'

A few seconds later Arend was looking at two identical copies of his own glamor.

'Idiots,' he sighed. 'Not exactly the same as me. Obviously. Make your own versions. And, Mist, yours should be female.'

Shaking his head, Arend took a cellphone from his pocket and, dividing his attention between the road and the screen, pulled up some images of ramp models, both male and female. He handed the phone to Mist. 'There, use those images to form your own simulacrums.'

A few seconds later the Range Rover contained three perfect, blonde and almost impossible beautiful humans.

If the *Hulder* really wanted to blend in they would have assumed more average countenances. But their natural hubris and arrogance meant they could only conceive of assuming what they considered to be the most beautiful and desirable of forms. Anything else would be below them.

So, they now looked decidedly human. Albeit in a Nazi pinup poster kind of way.

But they did not blend in. In fact, quite the opposite.

Arend knew this. But he didn't care. Far be it for him to assume aught but the most superior of simulacrums. He was, after all, *Hulder*.

Nodding in satisfaction he explained their next moves.

An hour later the three of them walked slowly through the rooms of the Museum de Toulouse. The huge, natural history museum situated in the center of the city. The group attracted much surreptitious attention as they moved from room to room. Appreciative glances from both men and women.

Using one of the free maps you picked up at the entrance, Arend led them to a specific display. In a glass case, laid out with accompanying plaques and explanations, was a full set of armor and weapons alleged to have been owned and worn by none other than King Euric.

Lamellar armor, a short sword, leather trousers. A selection of bracelets, greaves and rings.

Arend lay his hand on the glass case and concentrated, pushing his senses into the display. After a few seconds he nodded.

'The ring and the sword,' he said. 'The rest is not Euric's. In fact, the armor is almost a hundred years too late.' He glanced around the room, noting the old security guard and the other patrons. Then, with a casual flick of his wrist, he smashed the glass case and removed the ring and the sword.

The guard started from his state of semi-reverie and shouted out.

'Take care of him,' commanded Arend as he walked back towards the entrance.

Mist raised her hand and projected a bolt of lightning at the guard, striking him in the chest and killing him instantly.

'Idiot,' snapped Arend. 'Not like that. I told you, no magic. Next time, use your fists. Moron. Come on, we need to move.'

And with that, the trio left the museum, ran to the vehicle and headed back to Arend's abode.

CHAPTER 50

Jebe took his king's command seriously. As such, he put together a top team to find and destroy the Daywalker.

Five members. Two of the deadliest Chernobyl brethren and three familiars. Each familiar was ex Spetsnaz Russian special forces. All three had been dishonorably discharged for crimes against humanity. This for a unit that famously practiced its killing methods on live prisoners.

And the vampires had many centuries of fighting experience between them.

But Jebe knew, if the Daywalker turned out to actually exist, then he needed the most vicious and deadliest of warriors to take her down.

The familiars were kitted out with the very best equipment including state of the art lightweight nanotech body armor, custom made modern versions of the De Lisle carbine, a semiauto submachine gun that was almost completely suppressed. Almost as quiet as Hollywood movies would have you believe guns can sound. Added to this, a variety of bladed weapons, garrotes and small grenades.

The vampires, both just below Master level, carried no weapons. Obviously, they had no need to.

As well as the two vampires and the three humans, Jebe had, after much careful contemplation, added a Grinder to the team. A Grinder was a version of a vampire that had survived the turning process, but during the change their brains had been fried. Irreparably damaged by the virus that changed a human into a *Nosferatu*.

They ended up with the strength, speed and healing traits of the full vampire, but their intellect was little higher than a five-year-old child. A completely psychotic, ultra-violent five-year-old child with an insatiable hunger for human blood and a lust for battle.

Usually, Jebe would never have considered attaching a Grinder to a precision attack team. At best, the damaged brethren were used for large scale battles, house security, or sometimes they were set against each other in gladiatorial battles for the higher vampire's amusements.

But this Grinder was different. And unlike others of his kind he had even been gifted with a name. The brethren called him, Iscat. Russian for *The Seeker*.

Because this particular Grinder had gained an uncanny ability to track both smells and personal auras over vast distances, even after many days or even weeks had passed. Unfortunately, Iscat came with his own set of problems. He would have to be muzzled at all times and kept on a collar and lead. Basically, treated like a rabid dog. But in return he would give the team every opportunity of finding the Daywalker.

If she did indeed exist.

'You will proceed to the address I have given you. It is on the outskirts of Paris,' commanded Jebe. 'There you will find the burned out remains of a villa. It was owned by Pytor Smirnov.'

'The food guy?' asked Yelena.

She was the senior vampire on the team. Once she had been beyond beautiful, but in a cruel twist of fate, she was now one of the most hideously deformed of the Chernobyl victims. Tumors shaped like Shitake mushrooms covered her face, leaving only room for her mouth and eyes. Slabs of muscle looked like they had been applied by a poor plasterer, mounded on like raw concrete. Her strength and speed were off the chart, even amongst the monster vampires from house Belikov.

But because the gods have a cruel sense of humor, her voice had remained the same as before. A light, girlish, breathy tenor. A voice that brought with it visions of summer days and light cotton frocks and the smell of fresh cut grass. As opposed to the living nightmare from which it now issued.

Jebe nodded. 'The food guy. Yes. Along with the villa, Smirnov, his detachment of guards plus Leonid and Karl and their entire team were burned to the ground as well.'

'That must have been some firefight,' noted Igor, the second in charge. 'Hundreds must have been involved. I'm surprised it isn't international news.'

Jebe raised an eyebrow, an expression that was difficult to see through the ridges of scar tissue and lumpen nodules of flesh. 'There was no firefight,' he said. 'We believe the entire host was taken out by a small team. Perhaps two or three. Maybe even by a single protagonist.'

There was a rumble of disbelief amongst the team, but one look from Yelena and it ceased immediately.

Jebe waited for the team to settle. Then he dropped the bombshell on them. 'We think it may have been, the Daywalker. We also suspect that she may have teamed up with the new Omega, the one who replaced the last one after he died in the United Kingdom battle. This is all extrapolation, but regard it as truth. Be prepared.'

This time, even Yelena could not stop the team from breaking into discussion and statements of incredulity.

Again, Jebe waited for them to calm down. 'Questions?'

No one asked anything. There was no real point. If it was true, it was true. If it wasn't, well, then it wasn't. No use gainsaying or second guessing. It was time to travel to France and get

some concrete evidence.
   Finally, Yelena spoke.
   'How soon can we leave.'

CHAPTER 51

Crystals have power.

Not in the tree hugging, airy-fairy way that some proponents of the latest New Age religion would have you believe. No, crystals channel power. Not wishful thinking or positive vibrations. Actual magical power. Runic and thaumic energy.

Spells cast through the correct crystals will be both distilled and augmented. They are like an amplifier for a public address system.

But if you don't know magic, well, then they are simply shiny bits of rock.

Arend did know magic. Loads of powerful, reality altering amounts of magic. For he was *Hulder* and he was centuries old, and he was a kick ass mage of note.

The *Hulder* trio were currently traveling through the countryside outside of Toulouse. Arend drove, Remer sat in the back and Mist rode shotgun. But instead of a weapon, she held a seven-inch-long rod of Topaz, around twice the thickness of her thumb. The crystal rod had been cut and polished so it reflected every tiny bit of light and refracted it back in an orgiastic display of color. If one looked closely one could see the delicate runes cut into the surface. Hundreds of them. And one would also note that the crystal vibrated slightly, thrumming with latent power.

But this was not the power of destruction, this crystal was laden with the power of the hunt.

The *Hulder* called it a Seeker Wand.

It was currently seeking the grave of King Euric.

Well, to be completely accurate, it was actually tracking down anything that was part of the king or had been in his possession for any length of time. But Arend was confident it would lead them to the final resting place of the king. He had charged the wand using the items they had stolen from the museum. Like you give a bloodhound an item of a person's clothing so they can track them down.

'Left,' instructed Mist.

Arend frowned and checked his SatNav. If he followed Mist's instructions he would have to drive across through a fence, across an open field and ford a stream. Instead, he kept going to the next turnoff.

'Left some more,' insisted the female *Hulder*.

'I know,' snapped Arend. 'I'm not grotesquely stupid. I can follow simple directions.'

Mist frowned. 'I'm only repeating the wands prompts. No need to chew my head off.'

Arend took the next sideroad left, a mere dirt track. He slowed down and proceeded for half a mile or so.

'Right,' said Mist, pitching her voice so it appeared more a request than an instruction. Obviously attempting to lighten the atmosphere.

A minute later, she pointed at a small cottage that stood alone, next to the track. 'There.'

Arend smiled and pulled the Range Rover over. 'Let's take a closer look,' he said as he cut the ignition and got out.

The two compatriots adjusted their glamours and followed.

'Remember,' said Arend. 'No magic unless I give instruction or permission, and no dorky language.'

'Dorky language?' questioned Remer.

'You know, I've already told you. Foul metal, horseless carriage, noble steed. That sort of crap.'

Neither Mist nor Remer reacted. Mainly because they didn't actually know what he was going on about.

Arend held his hand out to Mist. 'The crystal,' he said. 'Give.'

She handed it over. Arend grasped it lightly in his right hand, stopped walking and pointed it at the ground as he turned in a slow circle. As he was dousing, a man came out of the cottage and walked towards them. He held an ancient double-barreled shotgun in his right hand and he

247

strode towards them with a purpose in his step.

'*Puis je vous aider?*' he shouted aggressively. '*Ceci est une propriété privée.*'

Arend scowled and turned to face the irate Frenchman. Pocketing the crystal wand, he muttered an incantation, combined it with a series of small gestures and unleashed a spell. But it was not aimed at the Frenchman, it was pitched to be cast on the trio of *Hulder*.

'Get off my land, intruders,' yelled the man.

Arend smiled. A universal translation spell was not an easy magic to perform, and he had just done it with ease.

Both Mist and Remer looked at him with respect. Both were low level mages, their warrior aspects being their main strengths. But they knew enough about casting to appreciate the skill involved.

'We are searching for something of importance,' said Arend. 'We won't be long.' He turned away and continued dousing with the wand, vaguely amused at how irate this strange human was.

'Don't turn your back on me,' shouted the Frenchman. 'What are you looking for? Are you from the government?'

Arend ignored the man completely and concentrated on the crystal.

The man raised his shotgun and pointed at Arend's back. 'Answer me. This is your final warning.'

'Remer,' said Arend softly. 'This human is bothering me.'

Remer nodded, drew a small obsidian throwing blade from his jacket and launched it using a deft underarm flick.

The blade struck the Frenchman in the neck, piercing his jugular and lodging in his spine.

The man dropped his shotgun as he grasped at the shard of obsidian, the look of surprise on his face so complete it was almost comical.

'*Merde*,' he whispered. 'I have been killed by a fashion model. How humiliating.'

He pitched over, dead before he hit the ground.

Arend continued his search. After a minute, he pointed. 'There,' he said. Then he strode back to the Range Rover, opened the tailgate and took out a pick and a shovel.

He handed the tools to Remer. 'Dig there,' he instructed the two compatriots.

They stared at him in shocked silence.

'Dig?' blurted Mist. 'In the ground,' she continued. 'Like a goblin. Or a dwarf. You cannot be serious. We are pure bred *Hulder*, not dirt grubbers.'

Arend took a deep breath, then he pointed at the patch of ground once more and, in a level voice, repeated the command.

'Dig.'

And he let a ripple of raw power flow from him. An expanding bubble of force that nudged both Mist and Remer as it washed over them.

249

Mist grabbed the shovel. Remer took the pick. They started digging.

Arend took out his ubiquitous clay pipe, filled it, lit up and lay back against a tree, staring at the lifeless body of the Frenchman. The rhythmic thud of the pick, counterbalanced by the slide and scrape of the shovel lulled him into a sense of peace. Contrary to the feelings of many of the *Hulder*, Arend actually liked the human world. He even liked some of the humans themselves.

They were a quaint race. Short lived but full of energy and ambition. Warlike to the point of ridiculousness. Even in the land of the Fae where most everything was decided by might of arms, there were moments of peace. But since Arend had started visiting the human plane, many hundreds of years ago, he could not remember a single period where some nation or tribe or faction was not warring against another one.

The human default setting seemed to be destruction. Truly, he mused, if you left a human alone for long enough, his one hand would declare war on the other.

His reverie was disturbed by Remer calling out.

'We got something.'

Arend walked over to the hole. At the bottom was something wrapped in a dirty, rotting bolt of what appeared to be linen. From the shape and size of the bundle it was obviously a body. That meant the wrapping would be a shroud. Unlike recent human history, in the time of Euric's reign, people were not buried in wooden boxes. They were shrouded in the finest linen and laid to rest with a few of their most treasured items.

'Remove the body,' he instructed. 'Carefully.'

The two compatriots lifted the body out of the grave and laid it on the grass. Using a blade, Arend cut the shroud away to reveal a desiccated corpse of a man dressed in full battle gear. Steel scaled armor, helm, rotting leather kilt, greaves and sandals. Next to him, a short Roman sword.

He waved the crystal wand over the body and it chimed with a clear ringing tone. This was most definitely King Euric. Or at least, it was when he was still alive.

But there was no sign of a necklace.

Instead, placed over the king's eyes, were two silver coins. The payment for Charon. The ferryman.

Arend could feel the power emanating from the coins as he leaned down and picked them up.

Roman Denarias, circa 33 AD.

Desperately he searched the rest of the body, tearing off the armor, shredding the linen. But they were no more coins.

He had proved correct. But he had also failed.

At least he had two more pieces of the fabled relic.

Now he needed to find the rest.

CHAPTER 52

The Morrigan floated in a sea of darkness. There was no sound. No light. The only sensation was that of cold. And weightlessness.

She didn't panic because she had been here before.

She was 'Between'.

For the last year she had been trapped – no, not trapped, *imprisoned* – in a world of pain. A world of heartache and regret and terror and every awful thing you could imagine. And all the while, she was unable to move. Her body frozen in time her eyes glued open, her mind assailed on a constant basis.

Imprisoned by a man she once loved.

Merlin.

The magician.

But it wasn't his fault. No, he had done this terrible thing to her at someone else's behest. Well, perhaps not their direct behest, but most definitely because of his misguided sense of loyalty to them.

Emily Hawk.

Shadowhunter. Daywalker, Gargoyle whisperer. Pack member.

Emily Hawk.

The font of all of the Morrigan's pain.

Of course, the goddess of war completely discounted the fact that she had betrayed her so called lover and led his dearest friends into a situation that resulted in their deaths.

And she conveniently forgot that Merlin had once before forgiven her for another betrayal. When she turned against King Arthur, causing not only his death, but the death of an era and a kingdom.

Because the Morrigan, or Morgana as she was sometimes known, was the embodiment of war. To her nothing else mattered.

The worship of the warrior was her entire raison d'être. Her sole purpose for being.

Anything that stood in the way of her goal must be destroyed.

And at the moment, that anything was none other than Emily Hawk.

The darkness around her shifted. Ever so slightly. The tiniest glimmer of light twinkled in the distance.

'Not long now,' she said to herself.

Then she smirked. It was ironic the only reason she had managed to escape her magical incarceration was thanks to the very girl she was looking to exterminate. If Emily hadn't cast her open mind out into the ether in an attempt to contact Merlin, then the Morrigan would not have had something to cling to.

But Emily was ignorant. Powerful beyond any other human mind the goddess had come across, but still youthful and callow. And she had no idea what risks she was taking by giving the entire universe a shout out.

The power of Emily's mind-shout was so strong it managed to pierce the veil Merlin had cast. The Morrigan had latched onto the thought like a limpet. And in doing so, it provided her with an anchor. A guiding beacon.

After that, it was a simple process of exerting her divine will and following the path of thought back to the earth's plane of existence.

Now she was close.

Another speck of light joined the first, and then another. And another.

Then, with a rush of sound and an explosion of color, the Morrigan found herself lying naked on a patch of bright green sod.

She took in a deep breath and knew instantly where she was.

The Emerald isle.

The seat of her original worshippers.

Ireland.

'*Tá mé sa bhaile*,' she cried out in Gaelic. '*Anois beidh vengence agam*.'

I am home. And now, vengeance will be mine.

All about her the land shivered in anticipation.

And fear.

CHAPTER 53

The darkness shrouded the two vampires with merciful cloaks of shade, hiding their obscene deformities in the inky blackness of the moonless night.

To the *Nosferatu*, the stink of charcoal and burned plastic and roasted flesh still lay thick in the air, despite the fact Smirnov's mansion had been burned down almost four days ago.

The Spetsnaz familiars could pick up the lingering smell of smoke, but the minutia of the other remaining odours was lost to them.

Iscat, the Grinder, on the other hand was slavering as he sniffed at the burned-out ruins.

Yelena had placed a stout leather muzzle over the Grinder's jaw, tethered a steel chain to his neck, and clad his hands in thick leather mittens. She had also hobbled him by connecting his legs together with a short length of chain. It was long enough to enable him to take short steps, but not long enough to allow free movement of any type.

Igor held the Grinder's chain and he led him around like a dog. Punching him in the side of his head if he hesitated to obey an instruction. Every time he did so, Iscat would whimper and then snarl at him, the hatred in his eyes as plain to see as a pair of headlamps on a clear night.

The familiars spread out, forming a perimeter around the ruins to prevent any unwanted attention from stray passers-by. Meanwhile, Igor pushed Iscat's head into the piles of rubble.

'Come on,' he encouraged. 'What can you smell? What's there?'

The seeker snuffled at the detritus left over from the fire, hunting for any scent that seemed unusual.

Iscat had no idea what he was seeking, but Igor had worked with him before, and he was confident that anything extraordinary, would set the Grinder off. Like a dog sniffing a mound of raw hamburger. Unusual scents, powerful auras of any kind. Something exceptional.

The Grinder shuffled from area to area, falling over every now and then as the hobble tripped him up. Whenever he stumbled, Igor struck him again.

After ten minutes, Iscat froze. His nose was buried in a mound of torn up carpet. He sniffed frantically and then let out an animal-like howl and whipped his head back and forth in an attempt to escape his collar.

'He's got something,' announced Igor.

Yelena ran over. 'What?'

Igor shrugged. 'Not sure. That's the problem

with using a seeker, you're never that sure what they're going after. But I've seen him take a scent before, and he's never been this excited. So, whatever it is, I guarantee it's well worth us following.'

'How does it work?' asked Yelena, who had never operated with a seeker before.

'It's easy,' answered Igor. 'Now he has their scent and the imprint of their aura, we can put him in a car, a train, even a plane, and he will always look towards the target. It's uncanny. I suggest we get back in the vehicles and simply follow, his nose. Literally.'

'Okay,' agreed Yelena. 'He's your responsibility. Let's give it a go.'

CHAPTER 54

Hadad held up the three coins. They had been joined together with links of pure silver and attached to a full-length necklace of white gold. There were another twenty-seven open links, in readiness for the rest of the Triginta.

He bowed ever so slightly as he handed the relic over to the king.

Belikov accepted it with shaking hands, his eyes glowing red with both greed and desire. He pulled the chain over his head and allowed the three coins to rest on his chest, directly against his mottled skin. As they touched his flesh, a crackle of electricity rippled across his body and a cloud of smoke rose towards the ceiling.

It took all of his control to stop from wincing as a wave of pain crashed over him.

And then it was gone, to be replaced it with a high of both physical and mental acuity. It was as if scales had been torn from his eyes and a weight lifted from his back. The feeling of power was almost overwhelming and he felt the need to stride forth and conquer. To rend his enemies and see them fly in terror before him.

To command.

To control.

He muttered to himself as he stroked the coins with his right hand, rubbing them softly between thumb and forefinger.

Hadad smirked to himself. 'Gollum,' he said under his breath.

Belikov stared at the philosopher. 'What?'

'Nothing of note, king,' answered Hadad.

'I trust that was not an insult you muttered, Arab.'

Jebe moved behind the philosopher and rested his hand on the blade at his hip.

Hadad raised an eyebrow. 'If you want to take it as so, then yes, I suppose it could be looked on as an insult,' he admitted. 'But an insult is a perceived thing. You can only be insulted if you allow yourself to feel insulted. Otherwise, it is a mere utterance of words signifying nothing but the thoughts of the utterer. Anyway, it was an observation, not an insult.

'Beware the power of the coins, king. Make sure you control them. They must never control you. Dominate them. Else they will dominate you.

'You can feel the unbelievable power imbued within, and this is but a tenth of the final relic. The full *Triginta* will be almost impossible to bend to your will. Even for one as powerful as you.

'You see, Blood King, that is how the curse

works. It kills through supplying a surfeit of power. So much so that it corrupts, it poisons. Much like the radiation released during the Chernobyl incident.

'But as you have all already been afflicted by such power, I would postulate that you are capable of overcoming the curse. Also, being undead tends to negate a death curse at any rate.'

Hadad chuckled, amused at the irony.

Both Belikov and Jebe stared at him like he was insane.

'You tread a fine line between usefulness and the true Death,' stated the king. 'Be careful you do not cross it.'

Hadad shrugged 'I will, or I won't.' he said. 'But as of now, I am still needed. Arend continues his quest for the rest of the Triginta. He is now searching for information on the people that buried King Euric. He theorises that one of them may have taken the rest of the *Triginta* and most likely broke it up to sell it on. Or perhaps one of the king's entourage stole it before that. Fear not, he will never stop searching.'

'And a team led by Yelena and Igor are searching for the Daywalker,' interjected Jebe. 'They have taken a squad of our Spetsnaz familiars and a seeker.'

Hadad frowned. 'A seeker? Why? They are notoriously unstable. Not to say untrustworthy. That is somewhat of a risk, don't you think?'

'You have a better way of tracking a subject

across the length and breadth of Europe?'

'Not sure,' admitted the philosopher. 'Perhaps a charm of some sort.'

'Pah,' scoffed Jebe. 'Magic and nonsense. No, the seeker is the correct choice.'

'If you say so,' conceded Hadad.

'Enough,' said Belikov. 'Leave now. I want to be alone with... I want to be alone.'

Both ancients bowed and left the room.

CHAPTER 55

The Professor tested the edge of the blade with a calloused thumb and nodded.

'Now stay still,' he said to Tag. 'I just want to stick this in your neck.'

'What?' yelled the big man. 'You mental or something?'

The Prof frowned. 'No. Maybe. Actually, that is a good question. After all, what is sanity?'

'Sanity is not wanting to stick a knife in someone's neck for no reason,' answered Tag.

'I have a reason,' countered the Prof. 'I want to time your recovery rate and map it against the figures we put together last year. I'm checking if your gift is getting stronger or weaker.'

Tag shook his head and turned away.

As he did so, the Prof stepped forward, plunged the blade into his neck and then pulled out an old-fashioned pocket watch and made a note of the exact time.

Tag fell to his knees, clutching at the blood gushing from his throat. Within seconds the flow of blood stopped and the big man got back to his feet.

The Prof scribbled some figures down in his note book.

'Crap,' shouted Tag. 'You ass, you ruined another one of my shirts. I ought to bop you one.'

Emily stood up and held Tag back. 'Stop,' she said. 'You know he doesn't understand. The Prof is obsessed with knowledge, stabbing you is just his way.'

'It'll be his way of getting bopped,' snapped Tag.

Emily grinned. 'Why? You're all better already.'

'Yeh,' admitted the big man. 'But it stings. Also, the shirts. That was my last one. And I don't care what those dudes at Tide say. It doesn't get blood out.'

'Tell you what,' said Emily. 'This afternoon, I'll take you to the Champs-Élysées, we'll find a fancy shop and I'll buy you as many shirts as you want.'

'As many as I want?'

'Sure,' said Em. 'Why not?'

'Twenty?'

'A hundred, if you want.'

'No, twenty is good,' said Tag.

As he started to strip off his sodden shirt, the door banged open and Merlin stalked in, his face pale with emotion.

'Bad news, I'm afraid,' he said. 'I have confirmed, the Morrigan has escaped her shackles. I suspect she has returned to *Éire*.'

'That is bad,' interjected the Prof. 'What do you suggest?'

'We need to move, soon,' answered Merlin. 'I have a place in the mountains, near Mont Blanc on the Italian border. It is well protected. I think we should leave as soon as we can.'

'Can't,' said Tag. 'The girly and I got shirts to buy. We can go after that.'

Merlin scowled at the big man. 'Tag,' he said. 'I hardly think the ire of the Goddess of War can compare to the frivolity of purchasing a few items of clothing.'

'It's not frivolous,' argued Tag. 'It's a necessity. Specially if that Boggart keeps stabbing me for his research.'

Merlin glanced at the Prof who shrugged.

'Pack,' commanded Merlin. We need to get to Mont Blanc as soon as possible.

'We can plan what to do from there, but I tell you this; we are looking at a continent-wide struggle. And this one might very well be harder and cost us more than the last one.

'It's time to gather the troops. It is time to prepare for battle.'

Emily blanched as she recalled the death and destruction and the heartache brought on by her last war.

And she wondered if she would be capable of living through such terrible loss and despair once more.

But she knew she would, because she had to.

For Emily Hawk knew …
Only the dead have seen the end of war.

Author's Note

Well, that's it … again. Emily and her boys are back in the mix. I assume, that's the problem with evil. As it is always said – *Evil is legion, and good is…well…not so legion, I suppose.*

Seriously, it's never easy being the good guy – but someone has to do it.

I hope you enjoyed the book. If you would like to discuss anything, or maybe even simply get hold of me to toss a few insults, my personal e-mail is zuffs@sky.com give me a shout, I promise I will get straight back to you.

Or, if you would prefer, hit this link. It will take you to my author Facebook page. Give it a LIKE and then whenever a new book comes out – or I have something unbelievable witty to say, you'll get notified.

https://www.facebook.com/craigzerfauthor

Thanks again for all your support.
Your friend in words – Craig.
EMILY SHADOWHUNTER 6
DOMINATION
should be out soon.

If you would like to take a look at some of my other books – here's yet another link!

This takes you to my Amazon Author page…

happy days.
https://www.amazon.com/Craig-Zerf/e/
B0034Q97JW/
ref=dp_byline_cont_pop_ebooks_1

For those who might like to read my HEX series. Here is a chapter...just a bit of a taste test!

CHAPTER 1

Man, this dude was persistent. As dumb as a sack of horseshoes, but as relentless as a mosquito. I had killed him twice already today, hoping that he would take the hint and stop following me. But it looked like it was gonna have to be wooden stake time. Or maybe a simple beheading.

That's the problem with vampires, they just don't know when to quit. Not that I blame them, you try going on a liquid protein diet for a couple of hundred years and see how bright-eyed and bushy-tailed you feel.

But this particular bloodsucker was starting to get irritating.

And irritating Sholto Gunn tends to be a life shortening career choice. Or, in this case, an *afterlife* shortening one.

First, I needed to find out why he was trailing me so determinedly. Ducking through the casino and exiting through one of the side doors that led to the carpark, I headed to the steps.

Readying myself as I walked, I rolled my shoulders and flexed my fingers. The thing with vamps is, they are fast. And I mean, shit outa a goose fast. You gotta take them hard and without warning, or you find yourself in a one-to-one situation with a streak of lightning. And that never ends well.

As I reached the top of the stairs, I palmed a spell cartridge in my right hand, turned the corner and spun around, dropping to one knee as I did so.

Sure enough, mossie boy was right behind me. Chucking the spell at him I released its power in the form of a binding conjuration.

'*Ligabus*.'

Ropes of air wrapped him tight as a tourniquet, and I felt a slight burn of energy flow through my chakra brands as they helped to channel the power. He keeled over and lay on the concrete floor. He made no attempt to shake loose because he knew, when Sholto Gunn spelled you there was no getting out.

'Hello, Hex,' he greeted. 'You going to kill me again?'

'You don't get to call me that,' I snapped at him. 'Only my friends call me Hex.'

He looked puzzled. 'But you have no friends.'

'How do you know?' I asked him. 'For all you know, I got tons of friends.'

He shook his head. 'No. Everyone thinks that you're an asshole. It's a universally accepted truth.'

It was pointless arguing with the bloodsucker.

After all, he was pretty much correct. It's hard to be a kick-ass magical enforcer and mister nice guy at the same time. Particularly when, like me, you aren't too fussy about who you work for. It's not that people hate me, it's just that I make them feel uncomfortable. A bit like having a red-headed step child.

'Why you following me?' I asked.

'You're in Vegas.'

Shaking my head, I repeated the question. 'I didn't ask you where I was, blood boy. I asked, why you following me.'

The vamp looked puzzled. Which was sorta a default expression with them so I didn't read much into it.

'Someone always follows you when you're in Vegas,' he continued. 'On account of your gambling ban. The syndicate insist that someone keeps an eye on you twenty-four seven whenever you're in Sin City. I thought you knew that.'

Of course, I knew about the ban, and the fact that the casino bosses always put someone on my tail whenever I hit the city. But it was usually a normy. A mundane. Someone outside of the paranormal spectrum. A down-at-heel gumshoe with a bad trench coat, a fedora, and a cheap suit.

Not a vamp. Although vamps made sense. In Vegas, you could move from hotel to hotel in a blacked-out limo and once inside, well, it was always night time. So, the old, burst-into-flames-in-the-sun thing didn't really come into play.

And they were like the bloodhounds of the paranormal world.

'Why you?' I asked. 'Why not a run-of-the-mill shamus?'

'You always give them the slip.'

I shrugged. That was true. The thing is, I often didn't even mean to, but that's the problem with being a wizard. Or any of the paranormal stable. Mundanes tend to overlook us if they lose concentration for even a moment. There, then gone. It frustrated the hell out of them.

Personally, I thought it was hilarious. They'd be following you, then glance away for a moment. Next thing, Laurel and Hardy style double takes, rubbing of eyes, and frantic swiveling of heads as they wondered where the hell you had disappeared to. Even though you were still right in front of them. Something to do with residual magical glamor or some such shit. I don't claim to understand it. What's the point?

'So then,' continued mosquito boy. 'You going to shoot me again?'

I shook my head. 'Nah. This time I think it's the true death for you. Bit of open heart surgery with a wooden stake.'

The vamp went pale. Which is quite a feat, let me tell you.

'Mercy?' he croaked.

'I'm only fucking with you,' I assured. 'No harm no foul. Look, go back to the syndicate. Tell them I'm adhering to the ban and I'm only in town to collect from Charlie Dancer. He borrowed twenty big ones from Tony 'No Lips' outta New York, and the vig is so high that if he doesn't pay up today, he's gonna be speaking Greek on account of the size of his national debt.'

The vamp nodded. 'Will do. And thanks, I owe you one. Rumor has it that Dancer is staying in the Balton Hostel. You know the place?'

I nodded. 'Yeah. Pile of crap past Freemont street. When did Dancer go so down-market?'

'Since he crapped out at the tables. Even bet his watch.'

'Cool. Thanks.' I headed for the stairs, keen to get to the hostel as soon as, lean on Dancer, and then blow this town. Let's face it, Vegas is a shit hole if you're not allowed to gamble.

'Hey, Hex,' shouted the vamp as I walked away. 'Still tied up here.'

'The bonds will degrade in another couple of hours,' I told him. 'Consider that your punishment.'

'Asshole.'

'Yeah,' I agreed. 'And then some.'

Chapter 2

Dancer was terrified. And rightly so. I'd been paid by Tony 'No Lips' to retrieve his money or, if Dancer didn't have the wherewithal, then I had to punish him.

I deduced that, as the lowlife was currently renting a bed in a shared room with six other people in a damp, shitty hostel, he was fresh outta dough.

'Please, Hex,' he whined. 'I'm begging you. Give me another couple of days. I'll see 'No Lips' right. I swear.'

'Don't be a dick, Dancer,' I replied. 'How you gonna raise forty-two large in a couple of days?'

'Forty-two,' exclaimed Dancer. 'I borrowed twenty only a couple of weeks ago.'

'What can I say?' I asked the lowlife. 'The vig's as high as a bum's body odor. You knew when you took the loan.'

'But I thought that I had a system,' whined Dancer. 'Roulette. It worked every time. Then when I got to the casino, it worked for about an hour and then … nada. Didn't matter where I bet or how much. Not one red cent.'

'What's the system?' I asked.

Dancer came over all shifty, eyes darting back and forth as if the shitty room was full of people who were desperate to steal his stupid nonworking roulette system.

'Talk to me, Dancer,' I said. 'After all, your life

is in my hands.'

So, he told me his system. It was complicated. It was difficult to understand. And it worked. I know that it worked because I had used it before. Just one of the reasons I was banned from gambling in the gambling capital of the world. I also knew why it had stopped working.

'It's a good system,' I told Dancer.

He shook his head. 'Naw. Didn't work.'

'Bet you ten to one that it stopped working in the Bellagio.'

Dancer raised an eyebrow. 'Yeah. How'd you know?'

'They cursed you,' I told the hapless gambler. 'As soon as they saw your system they got their house wizard to hit you with a curse. A bit of bad-luck juju. All the bigger casinos have got someone, but the Bellagio's is the best. You were had, Dancer. Tough luck. Still, that don't butter no bread with 'No Lips'. I've been instructed to make an example of you. Something public and painful. Can't have the word on the street that 'No Lips' is soft on nonpayment.'

'You going to kill me?'

I shook my head. Truth be told, I wasn't sure what to do with Dancer. The dude was an idiot. But he had basically been conned by the casinos. They could have just banned him the moment they picked up on his system. But they didn't. Instead, they cursed him and let the poor sucker bleed his dumb ass dry.

If I was a different person, then I would have taken the issue up with the casinos. And by *different person*, I mean, *incredibly stupid person with a death wish*. Because as mean and kick-ass, as I considered myself to be, one just didn't take on the might of the Syndicate without real good reasons. And Dancer's predicament simply didn't qualify.

After a few more seconds of deep thought I came up with a solution. Reaching under my jacket I took out another spell cartridge. About the same size and shape as an adult's index finger, the spell cartridge held enough power to channel any low or intermediate sized spell. I could double or even treble up on them if I wanted to raise the ante, but a single would be enough for what I needed right now.

Dancer stared with wide open eyes. Sweat ran down his face and he looked like he was going to throw up.

Grabbing his head, I smacked the spell cartridge against it and incanted the word as I did so.

'*Morbus.*'

Dancer shuddered as the spell took and then he started to keen as if in unbelievable agony, dropping to his knees as he did.

'Stop it,' I yelled at him. 'It's not that painful. Get a grip.'

After a few seconds, he managed to stop blubbering and looked up at me. 'What did you do?'

'You may wanna look in a mirror,' I answered.

274

'But be prepared, you ain't gonna win any beauty pageants.'

Dancer stood up and staggered across the room to the dull, chipped mirror in the corner. He took one look and started his blubbering again.

'Oh, come on, Dancer,' I said. 'It's just a few boils. I mean, would you rather be dead? Because that can be arranged.'

'I'm hideous,' he squealed.

'Yep,' I agreed. Well, I couldn't exactly argue. He was looking in a mirror and he did look marginally hideous. I'd hexed him with boils. Boils on top of boils. He looked like a cross between the elephant man and a bowl of lumpy custard. But on the plus side, I had put a slight spin on the hex that meant that he'd feel no pain. Yeah, I know, sometimes I'm all heart.

'How long?' he asked.

'That's up to you,' I shrugged. 'For every ten grand you pay back, you lose a few pustules. For every week you don't pay, you gain a few. I suppose you could say that it's now a competition against the carbuncles.'

'You're an asshole, Hex.'

'Yeah,' I replied. 'Been hearing that a lot lately. Have fun, boily-boy. Keep in touch.'

Taking the first cab I could find, I headed straight to McCarran airport and boarded the next flight back to New York.

Back home.

3

My apartment is in the eaves of the Dakota building. It's next to Central Park. Take a look when you're in the neighborhood. It's a well-known landmark and you can't miss it. It was built back in 1884 and the eaves apartment has been in my family's name ever since then. In fact, it's the only thing that I have that has anything to do with my family. A two-bedroom, two-bathroom apartment with one of the best views in New York.

My biological family that is. Both father and mother are missing presumed dead. I was brought up by Father Cooney and a bevy of sisters at the *Church of the ladies of the Cedars of the Lebanon*. It wasn't officially an orphanage, but then I wasn't officially an orphan. I was tutored by sundry priests and nuns. I met other kids as and when Father Cooney took me with him to visit the people of his parish and, all in all, I had as normal a life as one could, given the circumstances.

Until I turned sixteen.

Then things got weird.

Look, I might go into that all later. Suffice to say, eight years later I'm a recognized kick-butt hex-swinging mage of the highest order. I don't see Father Cooney much anymore on account of the fact that I do the odd bit of … well, maybe more than odd bit … of work for the dark council. The Brotherhood, as they call themselves.

But on the flip side, I also do jobs for the Council of Light. And if I ever do any work for the Holy Church. Well, I don't charge. Only for expenses. And, to be fair, I hardly inflate those at all. Never more than fifty percent, anyway.

But what the holy Father doesn't realize is, if I didn't do the work for the Brotherhood, then someone else would. And if someone else was doing it, well then, we wouldn't have any insight into what they were doing. I'm not saying that I'm any sort of moral double agent or nothing. Far from it. I'm just saying ... you know.

But Father Cooney is all, like–heathen devil-worshiping bastard, get thee hence.

Ah well, win some, lose some. Maybe someday the old coot will come around. I hope so.

Opening the front door, I entered my apartment. The entrance hall stretched before me and out into the near distance. The ceiling was over twenty feet high and two massive chandeliers lit the area with an orgy of rainbow-driven light.

Oh–didn't I mention that my cozy little two-bedroom apartment was only a two-bedroom apartment from the outside.

Once you were inside it was a fucking mansion. Twenty bedrooms, maybe more. A ball room, a gym, an indoor shooting range, a pool, a library. Servants quarters. Yeah, suck on it, Bruce Wayne.

To be honest, I'm not sure how the whole

Tardis effect works. Something to do with inter-dimensional space. Or is that transdimensional? No, wait, pandimensionable. Whatever, the inside of the apartment exists in a different dimension to the outside.

'Master Sholto?'

It was Grogoch. I called him Grog. Strictly speaking that wasn't his name as much as his species. Half-man, half-fairy. Originally from Scotland but arrived in America via a few hundred years in Ireland. Traditionally, the Grogoch tended to dress in twigs and moss and leaves and shit. But Grog was always in an old-fashioned black frock coat, olive breeches and shoes, with a green derby hat, and a pipe that I've never actually seen him smoke.

Strictly speaking, Grog referred to himself as my butler. But in reality, he served no man. I saw him more as a *consigliere* that took care of me as well as giving me his uncensored advice.

'Home again, home again, jiggety jig. Good evening, Grog,' I greeted. 'Another day another dollar. How goes? Everything watertight and tickety-boo?'

'Indeed, sir,' he answered in his rough brogue. 'News on the street is that you hexed Dancer something terrible. Well done, master.'

'Needs must, Grog.'

'To be sure, master. Unfortunately, no rest for the wicked, sir. The Dark Council want an audience with you as soon as possible.'

'Well, they are going to have to wait until tomorrow,' I informed my man-servant. 'I need a shower, something to eat, and then about twelve straight hours of shut-eye.'

'The shower and food are doable, sir,' informed Grog. 'But I advise that you forego the sleep for a while and rush yourself on over to the Brethren as soon as. They were hot to trot and I, for one, would not keep them waiting.'

Taking Grog's guidance, I had a quick shower, changed my clothes, bolted down a sandwich and went downstairs to hail a cab.

Half an hour later I was entering the massive office building that housed the central nervous system of the Brethren. Their offices, storage rooms, and, for many of them, their residences. Most people thought that the black-windowed sky scraper housed a bank. And it did. But it also housed so much more. And much of it evil. Although probably not nearly as evil as the bank that provided cover for the organization.

There was a side door that only paranormals could see and it was through this that I entered. To any mundanes it simply looked like part of the wall. Once inside, the security seemed disarmingly lax. But I knew different.

The power of the magical wards that were protecting the area were easy to divine, raising the hair on the back of my neck like a wave of static electricity. Thing with wards is, they don't work so well against me. Why? Because I'm a seriously kick-ass mage ... thought that we already had that clear.

Okay, there were also two trolls on the door. Seven feet and four hundred pounds of thick skin and pissed off. They were dressed in ill-fitting security uniforms and carried their traditional cultural weapons. Three-feet-long stone clubs.

Trolls were bad. I mean, a combination of evil, stupidity and immense strength, which is a particularly nasty blend. Plus, they had this unbelievably tough skin. Two inches thick and based on some sort of silicon element. Like rubbery rock. And these ones had been enhanced by the Brotherhood. Upgraded to be slightly less stupid and slightly eviler.

That's why I always carried my traditional weapon. A FN five-seven semiauto pistol that takes the latest 5.7mm ammo in 30 round mags. It's armor-piercing, as well as being silver-plated for werewolves, and thoroughly spelled for all other nasties. It even has a couple of milliliters of holy water in a tiny reservoir drilled into the back of each slug.

Because only a real mug relies on magic alone when it comes down to self-defense.

One of the trolls held out a wheelbarrow sized hand, stopping me from entering the elevator. 'Must check for weapons,' he rumbled.

'Fuck off,' I retaliated, my repartee as sharp as ever.

The heap of muscle looked puzzled for a few

seconds then he defaulted to type. 'Must check for weapons or I bash you inna head with my club.'

'You try, bridge dweller,' I said. 'And I'll shoot you in the face. Now, fuck off. I have special permission to carry.'

As it happens, I do have permission to enter both councils under arms. But I was sure that this heap of brain death probably wasn't in the loop. Still, not my problem. No one tries to disarm Sholto Gunn and lives to tell the tale.

The second troll hulked forward. Backup.

'Must submit to full body search and leave weapons at desk,' he added.

'Well, I'm a wizard,' I argued back. 'And some of my spells I can do using brain power alone. So that would make my brain a weapon. Do you want me to check that in at the desk as well?'

I could almost smell the circuits in their tiny minds burning as they processed the argument.

Eventually the leader shook his head and raised his club. 'I count to one then I smash your skull, or you let me search for weapon.'

'You're meant to count to three,' I informed him.

He shook his head again. 'That too many numbers. I count to one.'

I nodded. 'Fine. Go for it.'

'One.'

I drew my FN and shot him in the face. He keeled over like a felled redwood, crashing to the floor, and twitching a couple of times before laying still.

I turned to the second troll. 'You want to count?'

He shook his head and ushered me to the elevator doors, bowing as I entered. I pushed the button for the top floor. The Brotherhood upgrades must be working with this one.

They weren't going to be well pleased with me when I got upstairs. They tended to frown upon knocking off their guards. But I wasn't going to back down. I mean, if I had a dollar for every brotherhood troll that I had shot … let's just say, I'd have five dollars. Okay, but still, how many trolls have you killed?

I am Sholto Gunn, for gnome sakes, and I don't take no shit from trolls.

The escalator doors opened into a reception area. Marble floors, tapestries, subtle hidden lighting. No pot plants. The Brethren didn't do indoor foliage.

Behind the reception desk, my perfect woman. And I mean that. She was everything that I desired in a woman. And, yes, I know, I tend towards the standard clichés. I can't help it. I'm young and dumb and … well … whatever.

She was tall, blue eyes, long blonde tresses, shiny red lips, and a figure to kill for. She even had a Cindy Crawford mole that was a part of my living doll fantasies.

Perfect.

Of course she was. She was a succubus. Typical Brethren, using a denizen of Hades to greet their clients. With an effort of will I scrubbed her glamor from my sight and opened my mind to her real visage as opposed to the vision she was projecting.

The thing with succubae is that they are basically vampires. It's just that they feed on sexual energy as opposed to blood. When you pierce their glamor what you get is your basic vamp. And, contrary to popular literature, vamps aren't super-gorgeous. Neither are they possessed of vast pools of charm and sophistication. Also, they don't sparkle in the sun. They burn the hell up. You see, a vamp is simply an apex predator. Fast, mean, and almost immortal. In return for those gifts of the hunt they give up any vestige of humanity, sense of humor, human empathy, and ability to do complex mathematical equations. Actually, I'm not that sure about the last one, it's just that pretty much every vamp that I've met is as dumb as a fish.

This one was average height, long black hair, pointy ears, thin lips, and oddly protruding fangs. Not an ugly, by any stretch, but definitely a far cry from the total hotness that I had seen when I entered. We'd met before. Many times. Her name was Eva and she had no idea that I could penetrate her glamor. As a result, I baffled the hell out of her. She was used to men, and women, swooning at her image, willing to do anything for her on the off chance that she would indulge them with some manner of sexual favor.

'Whatcha, Eva,' I greeted. 'How goes? I have been summoned, not sure by who. Message was left at my house to come as soon as. Any ideas?'

'Senior mage Dougherty wanted to see you,' she said.

Dougherty was a big deal in the Brethren. Number two in the hierarchy. I didn't know who number one was. And I didn't want to know. But for the number two, as it were, to be handling whatever this was, meant it was a big deal. Grog had been correct, as usual, when he had advised me not to blow off the meeting.

'Can I go through?' I asked.

Eva nodded. 'Oh, Hex,' she called out as I started to walk off. 'He watched the CCTV footage of you downstairs. You know. Where you unnecessarily killed the guard. And he is pissed at you. Watch your attitude with him. For your own sake.'

I winked at her. 'Trust me.'

The succubus shook her head and sighed.

Dougherty's office was at the end of the corridor that ran off the reception area. I knew it well.

I knocked and waited. He definitely wasn't a knock and enter kind of guy. Disrespect could very well earn you a fireball to the face. Or worse. So, I knocked. I waited. I knew that he wasn't that busy. After all, he was expecting me.

But there are games to be played in the corridors of power and one of those games is, the big cheese always makes the smaller cheese wait for an uncomfortable period of time when he comes calling.

But I ain't nobody's cheese.

I opened the door and walked in.

The man reacted like I'd just crapped in his soup.

'Sholto. What the hell? Don't you knock?'

'I did knock. But you chose to ignore me.'

'I wasn't ignoring you, young man, I was busy.'

'Too busy to speak?'

'Watch your tone of voice,' snapped the second-in-command of the Brethren. 'Remember your place. Also, what the hell do you think you were doing downstairs? Now we're going to have to grow another one in the vats, and we don't have an endless supply of troll-based nutrients.'

'Well, this time, why don't you add some brains to the mix, then I might stop putting them down? Anyway, it's an education, a practical demonstration of the Darwin Principle,' I answered. 'Namely, those dumb enough to attempt to disarm Sholto Gunn need to discover that they are at the end of a very short evolutionary road.'

Dougherty sighed. 'You know, boy,' he said. 'Your mouth keeps writing checks that your ability won't always be capable of cashing. Why don't you take that chip off your shoulder and think before you speak next time?'

'Thought and deed, uncle' I said to the second-in-command of the Dark Brethren. 'Thought and deed. It's part of my irresistible charm.'

Yep. Gasp, shock, horror. The right-hand man to the prince of darkness was my uncle. Well, not my actual blood-uncle, but close enough that I called him such. It's a long story. And, like many others, I will get around to telling it, sometime. But suffice to say, I owed mister Daley Dougherty big time and, while blood is thicker than water, when you got no blood family, then water will just have to do.

'What's the down low?' I asked.

'Big problems,' answered uncle Dougherty with a sigh. 'We got some imports muscling in on our territory.'

'Human or fae?'

'Human, the fae are still bound to their inner lands. As far as we can tell, it's three senior mages and maybe a few acolytes. They're from Africa. Dark Earth magic. Very powerful. We can't track them down. They're using some sort of shielding spell. Not even sure when they arrived, but they started to make themselves known around a week ago, already stolen a couple priceless artefacts from some of our Brothers. Apart from that, nothing too overt. But it's obvious that they are making a move of some sort. We can feel their vibrations. Also, I heard rumors they have already killed a few of the low-level street mages. Protection boys.'

The street mages were the basic ground level muscle for hire who worked for the more criminal elements. The equivalent of mafia thugs. Button men for the mob. The sort of guys who could arrange to have your garbage delivered, as opposed to picked up.

And for someone to openly take out a few meant that either they were insane, or they were supremely confident in their abilities. Or, worse case scenario, both insane and confident.

'How many have they taken out?' I asked.

'Not sure, a couple? Maybe a few.'

'How?'

'Apparently, basic attack spells. Burning, dismemberment. That sort of thing. Brute force stuff. Over the top.'

'A warning,' I said. 'Flexing their magical muscle. Not good. I mean, those protection boys aren't the sharpest tools in the box, but when it comes to basic muscle magic they are pretty damn respectable. Did the boys put up much of a struggle?'

Daugherty shook his head. 'Hey, I don't know the down low here, it's just stuff I've heard. But rumor says that they tried to fight back. There were signs of counter spells, but whatever they used just bounced off their attackers. We're talking master level stuff here.'

'So, what do you want me to do?'

Dougherty stood up. 'Find these interlopers,'

he said. 'And kill them. Make an example. The messier the better. Discourage anyone else from thinking that they can come over here and steal a piece of our action. The Brotherhood control New York and I want that written in neon.'

'It's what I do,' I said. 'The usual price?'

'Plus a bonus if you sort this out quick. Two weeks tops. We'll double your fee.'

I held out my hand and we shook. A binding contract.

'I'm your mage,' I said. 'I'll be in touch.'

As I left Dougherty called out. 'Hex,' he said. 'Be careful. These guys are heavy hitters.'

I laughed. 'So am I, uncle. So am I.'

4

Despite the savage injuries to her face, it was obvious the body laid out in the mortuary drawer was his sister. And, although he had already known it would be her, the loss hit him like a wrecking ball, taking his breath away and settling a dark blanket of grief over his shoulders.

'Looks like it was a mugging gone bad,' said the detective. 'Her jewelry, watch, and handbag were missing. Of course, we're presuming she had such accoutrements on her.'

'How did she die?'

'Stab wounds to the torso,' answered the detective. 'Her left eye was removed by the perp, postmortem. We couldn't find it.'

'May I see the wounds?'

The detective shrugged. 'If you want to, but I'm warning you, it's messy.' He gestured to the mortuary assistant who folded the sheet back to expose the rest of the corpse.

The man drew a deep breath. He had hoped against hope. But now he could see the exact shape and size of the wounds he knew what he was up against. Her liver had been removed. As had her navel and a patch of skin from her breast. The raw flesh standing out against the unblemished ebony of her perfect skin.

He pointed at the cuts. 'Her liver is gone. Also, here, and here,' he continued. 'Skin and navel.'

'Yeah,' admitted the detective. 'The perp was a real sicko. I'm sorry you had to see that.'

The man looked up at the detective. His eyes blazed with a mixture of anger and scorn. 'How could this possibly have been a mugging gone wrong?' he asked. His African accent thicker than usual due to the emotional stress he was under. 'Her eye, liver, skin. She has been desecrated for a reason. Surely, you can see that? There was method behind this killing, and I can guarantee that it, or something similar, will happen again. Soon.'

The detective's eyes flickered away, unable to hold the man's gaze. 'Look, mister,' he said. 'Don't try to read more into this than there is. I know that it's hard to accept the death of a loved one, but facts are facts. There is nothing to lead us to believe that this is anything else than a theft that escalated. Case closed. Trust me, at this current time the city cannot afford a panic about serial killers and methodical desecration of bodies. Why start one?' He pulled the sheet up, covering the corpse once again. 'Look, I'm sorry for your loss. Now we got some paperwork to do, loose ends to tie up and then you can be on your way.'

The African man shook his head but didn't answer. What was the point? The outcome had already been decided. The strange death of a foreigner in the city was not something that was going to rank highly on the to-do list of New

York's finest. All they wanted was to wrap the case up, ship the body back to Africa, and clean the case number off the whiteboard.

Efficiency trumps truth every time.

He followed the detective out of the morgue and back to his office.

5

A cab ride later and I was back at my apartment. Stripping off and falling into bed I slept for twelve hours straight. Late the next morning I awoke and stumbled through to the kitchen. Greeting me was a mountain of victuals. Breakfast ala Grog. *Id Est*, a platter of sundry deep-fried meats.

Heart attack on a plate with an after of acid reflux.

Eventually, stuffed to the gunwales, I pushed the plate away, managed to burp out the entire first verse of *Mary Had a Little Lamb*, lurched back to bed and passed out until nightfall.

Yeah, I know. *Acedia*. The seventh deadly sin. Sloth. Whatever, I was tired. And anyway, I work better at night.

I dressed in my usual nighttime attire. Dark charcoal Italian suit, deep red shirt, as dark as congealed blood, no tie. Ties were merely something for an attacker to grab hold of.

In a shoulder holster, my FN five-seven, two extra full magazines, and a bandolier of six spell cartridges. My last six I noted, reminding myself I needed to forge another batch as soon as. Preferably tomorrow.

Taking the escalator, I stepped outside and ordered a cab to Times Square.

The Dullahan Bar.

The go-to place when I wasn't sure what to do

next. The thing with the Dullahan is that it was inaccessible to mundanes. Well, strictly speaking that's not true. A paranormal could take one in as a guest, but a person without power would be unable to even see the entrance. It's bang next to Ellen's Stardust Diner, which does a great choc-chip pancake by the way. If you're a mundane then don't even bother to look for it. You won't find it.

To anyone watching, it looks as though we just walk into Ellen's but that's where it ends. We end up in the bar and you end up ordering a Jerry Lee Lewis wrap at seventeen bucks a pop.

The Dullahan is owned by a six-hundred-year-old Irishman by the name of Gan Ceann. His name literally translates to, without a head. And I suppose that's because Gan doesn't have one. A head that is. Well, he does, but it isn't actually attached. You see, Gan is the original Dullahan. Or Headless Horseman.

He doesn't carry it under his arm all the time. Instead, he plants it on a dinner plate in the middle of the bar counter while his body moves back and forth behind the bar serving drinks. And what a bartender that body is. Harry's bar has nothing on the Bloody Mary that Gan's body can mix up. And don't even mention his Long Island Iced Teas. Sublime does not do it justice.

'Whatcher, Hex,' greeted Gan's head, as I walked in. 'The usual?'

Nodding my agreement, I sat down opposite

the head. The body slid my drink over. Two fingers of Jack Daniels, one finger spring water, and three ice cubes. Exactly the way Frank used to drink it. Good ole blue eyes.

Toasting both head and body, I took a long sip. 'So, Gan. What's the scuttlebutt? Any big news on the street?'

'There's always some shit going down,' answered Gan. 'You looking for anything specific?'

Waving my empty glass at the body I waited for it to bring me a refill before I continued. 'Looking for new faces,' I said. 'Heavy hitters. Maybe African.'

'This Council or Brotherhood business?' asked Gan's head.

'You know I can't go into that,' I replied. 'But, as usual, I pay well for any info.'

'I'll put the word out,' promised Gan. 'You throw enough money about and one tends to get a response.'

The body brought me another drink and I turned to survey the room. Check out the clientele.

The place wasn't exactly bumping and grinding. It wasn't that sort of place. Large enough to never appear full but designed with enough character to feel cozy. A row of booths filled the far wall on the left of the bar, random tables and chairs scattered about the room, and then a few doors opposite that led to a variety of restrooms. Male, female, and others. Dwarves, for example, had their own restroom, dark elves tended not to ablute with any other species, and trolls and ogres needed outsize sanitary ware. In fact, the restrooms took up as much space as the bar itself.

The room itself was cleverly broken up into areas of dark and darker. Some of the booths had curtains drawn across and others didn't even have tables and chairs. They were simple stone slabs suited to both troll and ogre. But not for orcs.

Orcs weren't welcome. Not in this bar. Not in New York.

Why, you ask? Oh, come on. You've all seen Lord of the Rings. Well, Tolkien got it right, let me tell you. Orcs are bad and that's that.

As I perused the clientele it hit me. I felt his presence before I saw him. A palpable sense of power. In itself that wasn't too unusual. A lot of powerful mages can broadcast their presence like an amateur radio ham. It's just that most of us tend to cloak that power. Whoever this was, either wanted everyone to know, or he didn't care or, maybe, he simply had his mind on other things.

But the alarm bells really started to clamor when he walked in.

A little over six foot. Long, black leather coat. White T-shirt that made his skin seem even darker than it was. Black coffee with a hint of blue India ink. Worn but well-maintained jeans. Some sort of special forces military foot-wear. Wide shoulders that tapered to narrow hips. Well-muscled but not like a body builder. Muscle built from hard work as opposed to the sterile confines of a gym. His hair was cut close to his skull, nothing fancy, no design or shape. Simply, cut.

Could this stranger be one of the African mages that I had been tasked with finding?

Just in case, I subtly palmed a spell cartridge, stood up and headed in his direction. As I approached, two things became apparent. Firstly, the dude was even more powerful than I had first suspected. Maybe even more powerful than me. And, secondly, he had a real wild look in his eyes. Not unhinged or anything, more a combination of surprise and bafflement.

Deciding to revert to my usual bull-in-a-china shop technique, I approached and greeted him.

'Yo. Wassup, dude? You look like you just woke up from a bad dream, can I help?'

He turned to face me and, as he did so, I saw him visibly take control of his feelings, suppressing his emotions and throwing up a shield that hid his power. 'That man has no head,' he said.

'Not true, dude,' I contradicted. 'There it is. On the dinner plate on the bar counter.'

He nodded his acceptance and then cast his gaze around the rest of the establishment, taking in the many various denizens of the paranormal that frequented the place.

'And this bar is full of *Tokoloshe*,' he continued.

The word, *Tokoloshe*, was a new one to me. But I could guess by its context and the manner in which he said it, that it probably translated to something like, *ugly supernatural mother fuckers*.

'Well, it is The Dullahan,' I informed him.

'I thought I had entered Ellen's Diner,' he said. 'I was looking for a beef sandwich. How did I end up here with a man with no head and a crowd of *Umptyholi*?'

Another word I hadn't heard before. Still, once again, probably a similar translation. 'Our type of people often come here when they are seeking sanctuary,' I told him. 'A break from whatever they are doing. It is one of the few places in New York we can meet and greet without all the hassle it often brings with it. The wards must have picked up your need when you walked in to the diner and they redirected you here.'

'Our type of people?' he questioned.

'Yep. You know, wizards, mages, trolls, paranormals. The mystical set.'

He nodded. 'I see. This is a meeting place for witch doctors and their familiars. Never before have I come across this. New York truly is an amazing place.'

He held his hand out to me. 'Greetings,' he said. My name is Bhekumbuvusi Mpangazitha and I am pleased to make your acquaintance.'

My brain struggled to register and reproduce

his name, but there were simply too many vowels and consonants crammed into too small a space for that to happen. So, instead, I just stared blankly at him.

He smiled. 'My friends call me, Vusi.'

I took his hand. 'Cool, Vusi. My name is Sholto Gunn. My friends call me Hex.'

We shook hands the African way, reversing grip half way through. After, I showed him to a seat and introduced him to Gan's head. I wanted to spend some time with this stranger, feel him out and see if he was one of the people that I was looking for.

'What's your drink?' I asked.

'Brandy. Straight, no ice. Full glass.'

Gan's head acknowledged the order and his body served it up, at the same time freshening my drink.

'So, Vusi, what brings you to the Big Apple?'

He didn't answer for a while, settling back in his bar stool, his eyes blank, hiding his thoughts. Obviously making a decision. Finally, he spoke.

'I flew here from the Valley of a Thousand Hills in South Africa in order to identify the body of my sister. Even now she lies unattended and alone in a stainless-steel drawer at the city morgue. Murdered. Sent to her ancestors before her time. She actually died some three weeks ago, on the full moon, but it took me that long to organize a visa and get over here.'

Although he was cloaking his thoughts, I could

sense his pain as obviously as if he were beating his chest and rending his clothing. This was not one of the men I was looking for.

Neither Gan or I reacted for a few seconds. The clichés rushed to the fore. *I'm sorry for your loss. I'm sure that she's in a better place now. Time heals all wounds.* All of them too trite and hackneyed to be uttered. Instead, I simply put my hand on his shoulder.

'Sometimes life just sucks,' I said as I chinked my glass against his in a toast to his sister.

'Truly,' he agreed.

We ordered more drinks and the evening wore on. Vusi discussed his sister, his life in the hills of Natal, South Africa, and his amazement at the heaving city of New York. It was his first time out of Africa.

But his stories were tempered with caution. There was no mention of his training. His power. His craft.

I too gave him a précis version of my life. Strictly G-rated. Well, maybe PG. We both knew we were lying to each other by omission, but I figured that, as we were both complicit it was the same as not doing it.

Around midnight, Vusi opened up a little more. I suspect that the alcohol, the company, and the fact that he was surrounded by beings he insisted on referring to as, *Tokoloshe*, brought home he had no real reason to hide his powers anymore.

'What do you know about the *ingelosi iwile*?' he asked me out of the blue.

I shrugged. 'Never heard the words before.'

He frowned slightly, then carried on. 'You might call them, *idemoni*.'

'Demons?'

'Yes, demons.'

'Let's assume I know enough to hold a conversation,' I admitted. 'Why?'

'When my sister was murdered, the perpetrators took her left eye, her liver, navel, and a patch of skin.'

My stomach cramped. There was only one spell that called for those specific body parts.

Daemon Sublato.

Raising a higher demon.

And even the most psychotic, deranged member of the Dark Brotherhood wouldn't dream of casting such a spell. But there was no conceivable other use for such a specific shopping list.

'But why her?' I asked. 'Just bad luck?'

Vusi shook his head. 'She is of royal blood. My family are of the line of kings, albeit far from the actual throne.'

This fact made things worse. Worse by a factor of many. And more. If the spell of *Daemon Sublato* was performed with the inclusion of royal blood, then the demon that could be raised would not only be a higher one, it would also be a prince. A prince of darkness. To put that into perspective, the last time that demon princes walked the earth was during The Rebellion, when Lucifer himself was cast out of heaven for starting an argument with the Big Man.

Another description for Demon Prince would be–Fallen Angel.

So, some power-hungry nutcase was out there getting ready to attempt to summon one of the most powerful, most evil beings in the multiverse.

This was less than good news.

But there was one fact that was still in our favor. 'If memory serves,' I said. 'Don't the conjurers need another three sets of body parts? I must admit, I'm a bit hazy on the ritual, being of the thought that no one would ever actually use it.'

'Four sets,' agreed Vusi. 'One from each corner of the world. African, Asian, Caucasian, and Australoid.'

'Australoid?'

Vusi nodded. 'Basically, Australian Aboriginals. But it doesn't mean they have to be harvested in their actual countries. As long as that was their place of birth, the spell will work. My sister was murdered four days ago on the last full moon. That means the ritual will take place on the night of the next full moon. I have eight days to find these people and kill them.'

'Big ask,' I said. 'You don't have much to go on.'

'On the contrary,' said Vusi. 'When I saw my sister's body I picked up much residual magic.

Whoever did the murder was powerful, but clumsy. I would say, three men. All upper level mages. They used Dark Earth magic. And they were definitely from my home continent. They were Africans.'

Raising an eyebrow at this news I told Vusi about the task the Dark Brotherhood had set me. We both agreed that, in all probability, we were seeking the same people.

And that called for a few more drinks.

https://www.amazon.com/HEX-Book-Big-City-Magic-ebook/dp/B07D1SB4T9/ ref=rtpb_25? pd_rd_w=lvnQN&pf_rd_p=be844577-fee7-4bbc-8dda-083e56cc6f0d&pf_rd_r=6HT4 PS2RYYJKFCS5NMW3&pd_rd_r=9ee706dc-fd1f-46e8-aa3f-de16eb0d586e&pd_rd_wg=Uqfqw&pd_rd_i= B07D1SB4T9&psc=1

Printed in Great Britain
by Amazon

14361606R00173